PIANO MAN

PIANO MAN

by
Joyce Sweeney

Delacorte Press

Published by
Delacorte Press
Bantam Doubleday Dell Publishing Group, Inc.
666 Fifth Avenue
New York, New York 10103

Library of Congress Cataloging in Publication Data

Sweeney, Joyce.
    Piano man/Joyce Sweeney.
       p.   cm.
    Summary: Fourteen-year-old Deidre ponders the meaning of true
love as she deals with her enormous crush on the twenty-six-year-old
musician in the apartment upstairs.
    ISBN 0-385-30534-6
    [1. Love—Fiction.   2. Musicians—Fiction.]   I. Title.
PZ7.S97427Pi   1992
[Fic]—dc20   91-18410
                                                          CIP
                                                          AC

Interior design by DIANE STEVENSON/SNAP-HAUS GRAPHICS

Manufactured in the United States of America

May 1992

10 9 8 7 6 5 4 3 2 1

BVG

To Marcia Amsterdam,
the best agent in New York

PIANO
MAN

1

Deidre and Susie stepped from the air-conditioned building into the hot blast of afternoon. May in Florida was like August in the real world. Luckily, there were only two more weeks of school to endure.

"All right, what's the big news?" Deidre asked, shifting her books so *The Scarlet Letter* would stop poking her in the chest. She had found a note from her cousin Susie in her locker grating this morning that read, *The world is changed forever. Details at 3:00.*

"Okay," said Susie in her excited, hiccupy voice. "So Mom and I went to the mall to buy a graduation present for *Son*-dra and by the way, we got her a fourteen-karat gold figaro chain and I hope my mother remembers that! Because I better get exactly the same thing when I graduate high school—"

"What *happened* to you?" Deidre barked. She had no patience for the way Susie told stories.

"In fact, I don't see why I don't get a present *this*

year," Susie continued. She had no patience for Deidre's impatience. "I think graduating junior high is more important than high school. I think right now we're at the biggest turning point in our lives. Otherwise, we wouldn't feel so screwed up."

"Well," said Deidre, trapped against her will in one of Susie's irresistible arguments, "how do you know *Sondra* isn't feeling even more screwed up than you?"

"What's she got to be screwed up about?" Susie cried indignantly. "She's the one Mom likes!"

Deidre shifted her books again. "Maybe she worries about having a sister who hates her."

"I *don't* hate Sondra!" Susie said, shaking her head so emphatically, it whipped her short blond hair like a flag in a windstorm. "I just wish she'd never been born."

"Oh. Okay," said Deidre. It was too hot to argue.

"So Mom decides to head for Laura Ashley or one of those tea-and-crumpets boutiques to pick out a fox-hunting ensemble, and I didn't need that noise"— Susie's own taste ran to the neon and the stretchy—"so I struck out by myself and ended up in the food court—"

"Cruising," Deidre interrupted.

"I wanted a Coke!" Susie protested. "But when I got there . . . there he was."

"Mel Gibson," Deidre guessed. "Reverend Dimmesdale. The Apostle Paul."

"The most gorgeous male person who ever walked the earth!"

"Right there in the food court?" Deidre asked.

"Right there in the food court. The King of the Babes. The Ultimate Warrior."

"What was he doing?" Deidre asked. "Waxing the floor?"

"He was winding up a toy pig!" Susie said with a girlish giggle.

Deidre lifted her dark curls from the back of her neck and let the breeze blow through. "This is the most romantic story I've ever heard."

"He works at Embraceable Zoo. He had one of those little pigs, have you ever seen them? You wind them up and they walk around and say, 'Oink! Oink!' and the tail spins."

Deidre yawned.

"He set the pig on the floor and when he was straightening up he happened to look in my direction and our eyes locked and, I don't know, something happened."

"Oink! Oink!" Deidre said.

"It did! It was magic! Believe me!"

"I *can't* believe you, Suze. I believed you the last time when you fell for the guy who came out to enclose your patio. Remember? You thought something was really going on with you two. I was trying to figure out what to wear to the wedding. Then you found out he was married and had three kids."

"This is different," Susie said.

"I don't see how. It sounds like the same story to me, except for the toy pig."

"Okay," Susie said. "The difference is he asked me out."

Deidre's jaded facade cracked like ice on hot pavement. "He did?"

"He did," Susie said. Her blue eyes crinkled with amusement. "Are you still too bored to listen?"

"No, not really," Deidre said. What made this information especially stunning was that Susie had never gone out with anyone before and neither had Deidre, unless you counted group dates or the horrible social events sponsored by Ramblewood Junior High, where you had to dance with sweaty guys you'd known since kindergarten. "I guess you're leaving some of the story out," Deidre said. "I mean, one minute he's winding up the pig and the next you've got a date. What happened?"

Confident she now had a good hold on her audience, Susie took her time, shifting her tote bag to the other shoulder, running a graceful wrist up through her bangs, centering the gold *S* that hung from her neck chain. "Let me describe him to you first. He's sixteen."

"What?" Deidre squeaked. "Are you kidding?"

"No, I'm not kidding. He's a tenth-grader at Taravella."

"Does Sondra know him?"

"I'm not asking her about him! This is my own private, secret thing! If she knew I liked him she'd try to steal him. His name is Curt Wyler. He knows *her*, though. When he said where he went I said she was my sister and he said, 'Oh, the Ice Princess.' Don't you love it? I hope all the guys call her that! Anyway, then he said, 'I can't believe you're *her* sister.' *Tu comprends?* He's telling me *I* don't seem like any ice princess."

"Yeah, I *comprends.* Did he know how old you were?"

"Sure. I told him. He said, 'You seem really mature for your age.' He and I are perfect for each other, if you go by that thing about girls maturing faster than boys."

"I don't know if I do or not."

"I do. Anyway, he said, 'I'd like to take you out sometime,' and I said I'd think about it."

"At least you didn't say yes."

"What does that mean?"

"Well"—Deidre slowed her pace a little. They were getting close to Susie's house and this was important— "I mean, I have to admit this is the most major thing that's ever happened. But you were just having fun, weren't you? You wouldn't really go out with a sixteen-year-old, would you?"

Susie's gaze was frank and fearless. "Why not?"

"I don't know!" Deidre said. She didn't know. But it was obvious, wasn't it? There had to be some reason for all the warning lights and bells going off in her brain.

"If he thinks I'm mature enough to go out with him, that's good enough for me," Susie said defiantly. "But I want you to see him, before I make my final decision. He had on these tight black jeans and a shirt that must have cost—"

"Don't describe his clothes!" Deidre said. "Describe him!"

"Dark brown hair, the very shiny kind, you know? Brown eyes, great eyebrows, cute butt . . ."

"That about covers it. Well, do you want to go over tomorrow?"

Susie scrunched up her face. "Nope. Tomorrow's the day Sondra and I have to go to Delray and act like we still have a relationship with Dad."

"Tell him I said hi," Deidre said. She liked her uncle Jack. He was her mother's brother. Since he divorced Susie's mother it felt like the whole family had fallen apart. "Do you think Curt works on Sunday?"

"We can find out. I can't wait for you to see him."

"So if I think he's all right, you're going to go through with this?"

"Of course I am! I'll probably do it even if you don't like him. How could anybody turn down a chance this good?"

"I don't know," Deidre said, trying to imagine what she would do in such a situation. "I really don't know."

"I'll call you Sunday morning," Susie said, turning up her driveway. "Ciao!"

"Ciao," Deidre said absently. This was a lot to adjust to. It was exciting and scary, and it made her feel jealous too. Still, in a way, she was relieved it was happening to someone else. She could enjoy this interesting story without any possibility of getting hurt. And there was another feeling she couldn't quite identify. It was a little like . . . *grief.*

The breeze had died down by now. The horizon was hard and shimmery. Deidre shifted her books for the third time. The five blocks between Susie's house and home suddenly seemed like a thousand miles.

I

The first Post-It note was on the antique clock in the foyer. *Is this broken?* the note said.

"No, Mom," Deidre said aloud. "Just needs to be wound." She wound the clock and began searching the apartment for other messages. Every afternoon she went through this ritual. It was like a treasure hunt.

On the cupboard was a note that said, *We're running out of cereal.* On the refrigerator, *Let's have chicken tonight.* In her mom's bathroom there was water all over the floor and a note that said, *Watch it!* Deidre collected and threw away all the notes, mopped up the water, put cereal on the grocery list, seasoned a couple of chicken breasts and put them in the oven. When she went to her bedroom, there was a final note she had missed, posted on the mirror. *I love you.* Deidre smiled. "I love you too," she said. That one she decided to keep.

Deidre was a firm believer in doing the unpleasant things first and saving the best for last. If there was a nut in the middle of a cookie, she would eat all around the edges, making a glorious, final bite out of the center. In the same way she always did her math homework before her English. She studied her problems now, struggling to focus her mind on stories she couldn't care less about. *If a boat is moving downriver at 5 mph and a car is driving along the bank in the opposite direction at 10 mph . . .* Why would anyone want to know this, Deidre wondered. She got A's in every subject except algebra because she hated it so much. Algebra, she felt, didn't deserve any better than that.

Suddenly, she realized there was music coming from somewhere. It had been playing for a while, but she hadn't been consciously aware of it. It was coming through the ceiling from the apartment upstairs. Somebody was playing the piano! It must be the new person who moved in yesterday. Deidre had seen the van and watched the men carrying in furniture, hoping to get a clue about her new neighbor. But it had been the usual Haitian cotton sofa and wicker chairs everyone had in Florida. She certainly hadn't seen a piano. But she knew the music was live because of the way it stopped and started. The song this person was playing had the strangest effect on Deidre. It made her feel . . . *happy.* It gave her a happy, soaring feeling inside. It was like a waltz, sort of, but livelier, with long runs up and down the keys that were curiously thrilling. The person upstairs was playing the song with great feeling. Deidre put down her pencil to listen. It was kind of familiar. She knew she had heard it, on the radio or somewhere. An older song, maybe. It made her want to get up from her chair and dance, whirl around the room, sing, laugh, jump for joy! Timidly she pushed her chair back.

But the music stopped. Just like that. She waited hopefully, looking at the ceiling, but the apartment upstairs was silent. Slowly, she picked up her pencil again. *A man has a salt-brine solution that is two parts water to one part salt. If he adds enough water to . . .* Deidre had to swallow hard several times as she read this. Losing that song had almost made her cry.

I

"He grows orchids," Deidre's mother said, stabbing into her chicken. "Did you know they don't need dirt? They have an aerial root, that was what Mr. Maxwell called it. He takes them and hangs them, like, on the branches of *trees.* Can you imagine that? What did you do to this chicken, Dee? It's so good."

"Paprika and thyme," Deidre said absently. She tuned in and out when her mother was talking. Especially if the topic was Mr. Maxwell, the accountant her mother had just gone to work for. Deidre had nothing personal against Mr. Maxwell, since she'd never met him, but she'd already heard more about him than she wanted. She knew about Mr. Maxwell's divorce, Mr. Maxwell's trip to the Soviet Union last fall, and Mr. Maxwell's inability to digest milk products. Enough was enough.

"Paprika and thyme," her mother mused. "I

wouldn't recognize those things if they fell on me. Who taught you to use those on chicken?"

"I figured it out by myself," Deidre said. She knew she wasn't going to make her mother understand culinary intuition any more than her mother could make her understand the pleasures of mathematics. Deidre's mom, who was a bookkeeper, sometimes ran up imaginary figures for *fun*. "Do you know anything about music?" Deidre asked, trying to keep her voice casual.

"Oh, you know. What are you talking about? I don't know anything about classical music, if that's what you mean. Mr. Maxwell does, though. He and his wife used to go to the opera together. Can you imagine—"

"If I hummed a little piece of a song, do you think you'd know what it was? I think it's something from your generation."

"You can give it a try. I'll *try* to remember that far back." Her mother laughed.

It was difficult for Deidre to reproduce the runs and chords that made up the song, but she did her best.

"Oh, yeah, that's familiar," her mother agreed. "I think it's some old Billy Joel something. I don't know. It sounds like you're leaving part of it out. It's Billy Joel. Not 'Allentown' but . . . I don't know."

"Billy Joel," Deidre repeated. That was a place to start, anyway.

"Why did you want to know?"

"I just heard it today and I liked it. I thought I'd get a tape of it or something." Deidre decided not to say the music had come through the ceiling. Her mother might complain and get it stopped.

"Do you like my hair up or down?" Deidre's mother asked.

"What?"

"Up or down? Is my neck too long to wear it up?"

"No, it looks great that way. Why?"

"No special reason. Need any help with your homework tonight?"

"No, I did it when I first got home."

Her mother looked disappointed. "Okay. You sure are a trouble-free kid."

Deidre smiled and got up to clear the table. "Dessert?"

"What have we got?"

"There's some ice cream left. And I think we have some cookies."

"Let's have both. I'm really hungry tonight. Dee? I want to ask you something. Do you think it was all right for me to tell Mr. Maxwell to call me Janet?"

Deidre was in the kitchen now, scooping ice cream. She put down the scoop. "What?"

"I told him to call me Janet. Do you think that was okay?"

Very slowly Deidre dried her hands on a dish towel and walked to the kitchen doorway.

Her mother was looking up, waiting for Deidre's answer with a strange mixture of excitement and guilt on her face. She looked like a little girl asking something of a parent instead of the other way around.

Deidre folded her arms. "Why wouldn't it be okay? That *is* your real name, isn't it?"

Her mother blushed. "You know what I mean. It just sounded so funny, him calling me Mrs. Holland."

"Really?" Deidre said. "I've heard lots of other people call you Mrs. Holland. What's wrong with that?"

"You know! It's so formal!" Her mother tweaked back an errant lock of hair. "You know how much I hate that kind of stuff."

"Yeah," Deidre said. "Well, if he doesn't care, I don't care. You can tell people to call you anything you want, right?"

"Right!" her mother said brightly. "That's what I thought."

Deidre went back to the kitchen and finished dessert. She set the two bowls of ice cream and the plate of cookies on the table, then sat back down at her place.

Her mother attacked the ice cream ravenously, not meeting Deidre's eyes.

"Mom," Deidre said, "do you *like* Mr. Maxwell?"

Her mother's blue eyes flicked up briefly, then back down. "Sure I do. You know me. I like everybody."

"Yeah," Deidre said. The rest of the meal was eaten in thoughtful silence.

2

Deidre was bored. After they came back from the grocery, her mother had spread papers and pencils all over the dining-room table and was punching away ecstatically on her computer. It was, she had told Deidre during a Coke break, a financial plan for a very important client.

"You're really knocking yourself out to impress old Mr. Maxwell, aren't you?" Deidre had asked.

But her mother didn't answer. Her mind was lost somewhere in the astral plane of numbers. Deidre figured even if an armed gunman came in now and started shooting up the place, her mother wouldn't know.

Deidre picked up the TV listings. Pretty bad. It was Saturday afternoon, so there was nothing but baseball games and *This Old House*. Susie was in Delray pretending to have a relationship with her father.

"Mom! Guess what! I think I'm pregnant!" Deidre called, just to amuse herself.

No reply. Deidre sighed and went to the kitchen to look for food.

"Honey? Would you bring me something? I'm starving!"

"Mom!" Deidre cried, rushing into the dining room. "Was that you? Did you speak?" She picked up her mother's wrist and pretended to take a pulse. "Sit right where you are. I'm going to get a flashlight to shine in your eyes."

"What are you talking about?" her mother asked. "You're not making any sense. I just want something to eat."

"Okay," Deidre said, giving up on sarcasm. "What do you want?"

"Anything. Just a sandwich. Something I can eat fast." She glanced longingly at the computer again.

"Okay," Deidre said. "We won't keep those spread sheets waiting." She fixed two sandwiches and two glasses of milk and carried them in.

"Mmm," said her mother. "Your meat loaf is so good."

"I put chili sauce in it," Deidre explained.

"It's great. You have such a genius for food. Where do you get that? Maybe from my mom. You know what a great cook she is."

Deidre thought so, too, but she didn't like the idea of

"getting" her talents from other people. "I think it's something you're born with."

For the first time that day Deidre's mother really seemed to detach her mind from her work. She looked up with something feverish and excited kindling in her blue eyes. "Dee! You know what we should do? We should start showing you off a little. Why don't we have people over for dinner sometimes?"

Deidre was not fooled. Her mother always got excited like that when she was setting a trap. "Who would we have over?" she asked.

"I don't know. Your friends. My friends. Mr. Maxwell . . ."

"Mr. Maxwell!"

"He's a bachelor. I know he doesn't eat right. He skips breakfast and if he doesn't have a lunch meeting, he just eats a candy bar."

"How tragic."

"Well, wouldn't that be a nice thing to do?" her mother insisted.

"Yes, I guess it would. Do you want to do that?"

"Only if you'd be willing to. Then, some other time, we'll have a friend of yours. I mean, you're such a good cook and we have that set of china that never gets used. . . ."

"Yeah, you've definitely got a point. It scares me how we don't use that china. Okay, we'll start with Mr. Maxwell, since he's wasting away."

"Great! What would you fix for him?"

Deidre laughed. "What do you want me to fix?"

"Well, he's allergic to dairy products. I know he likes Russian food."

"I don't know any Russian recipes except beef Stroganoff. And that has dairy products."

"Oh. Well . . ."

"How about a pot roast? If he's a poor, lonely, miserable bachelor he should love that."

"Oh, perfect. You can fix it with potatoes and carrots and onions—"

"Yes, I know how to do it, Mother. I'll even bake biscuits. And something for dessert like chocolate cake, right?"

"Oh, that would be wonderful. Do you think he would come if I asked him?"

"He'd be crazy if he didn't. Are you going to buy a new dress?"

"A new dress? Why on earth would I buy a new dress just because I'm having my boss over for dinner?"

"Excuse me, Mom." Deidre laughed. "I lost my head."

∎

After lunch, the spread sheets took over again and Deidre felt like climbing the walls. She finally decided to go down to the pool. She really hated the pool on Saturday because it was usually dominated by the young singles grabbing at each other underwater, but Deidre felt she had no choice. Until that financial plan was done, she was a lonely, friendless orphan. She changed into her suit, wrapped up in a beach towel, and went down.

Surprisingly, the pool area was quiet. The young singles must have gone to the beach. There was only one man, a big guy in track shorts, sleeping in a lounge chair with a towel over his face.

Instead of getting in the water Deidre sat down in a deck chair on the opposite side of the pool and began putting on suntan lotion. Her motives, she realized after a minute, were not too honorable. What she was really doing was taking advantage of this guy's unconsciousness so she could look at his body. That might not be very nice, but it was a rare opportunity to really check a guy out from neck to foot without getting caught.

And he was quite a specimen to check out. He was tall and big boned, neither thin nor fat, just solid looking. His feet were long and narrow and his hands, one of which was hanging down, big knuckled and squarish. He was very tan, with a goldish fuzz on his chest and thighs, suggesting he was blond. The bottoms of his feet were very white.

The best part of him, Deidre decided, was the shoulder area. He wasn't musclebound, but his shoulders were broad and strong looking.

His shorts were striped to look like undershorts and the parts of him they covered looked all right too. In fact, there was a breeze blowing and it kept lifting the hem of his shorts on the right side, not quite enough that Deidre could get a glimpse of anything indecent, but coming close enough to make her think she'd better look somewhere else.

She decided to focus on clues to his personality, instead. His beach towel, for instance, the one covering his face, was a black-and-white Jolly Roger. That had to mean something. On the deck beside him was a pair of battered tennis shoes with the laces tied together, a bottle of expensive suntan lotion, a pair of neon-green sunglasses like you might get free in a cereal box, and a magazine, whose pages were blowing all around in the wind. The magazine, Deidre knew, was crucial. When she saw the magazine, she would know the man. She figured a guy like that would read *Sports Illustrated* or *Playboy* or, if he was intelligent, maybe *Esquire*. Something very male.

Deidre knew her worst flaw was curiosity. Once she started wondering about something, she could be obsessed in seconds. She felt she just had to see that magazine. But on the other hand if she went over there and he woke up, she would die a thousand deaths. She struggled with herself for several seconds, but she knew her rational side would lose. At least, she decided, she wouldn't be looking up his shorts.

Stealthily, she lifted herself from her chair, taking care not to let it creak. Feeling vulnerable, she wrapped her towel around her shoulders and slowly made her way around the pool, watching the man all the time for any sign he was waking up.

She circled behind his chair and leaned forward to look at the magazine. The trouble was, the pages were blowing around so much, she couldn't make anything out.

Deidre stood for a long time, making her decision. Then she crouched down, inches from the sleeping man, and reached between the two chairs. Her fingers began to tremble. At this close range she could smell his cologne, which was citrusy, mixing with the coconut scent of his sunscreen. He smelled like a human piña colada.

Fully extending her body, which was now rigid and shaking, she caught the edge of the magazine with two fingers and lifted it, so it wouldn't make a dragging sound on the cement. She held it up and looked at the cover.

Cat Fancy: The Magazine for Responsible Cat Owners. There was a picture on the cover of a striped kitten looking into a goldfish bowl.

While Deidre was getting over the shock of this, the towel beside her suddenly stirred and the man sat up.

Deidre screamed involuntarily and dropped the magazine. The man, still half asleep and finding a girl next to him screaming, screamed back. Deidre decided this was the worst moment of her life, worse than when she threw up in kindergarten. She could feel a raging blush spread over her face, burning all the way back to her ears. If she had decent reflexes, she would have put *her* towel over *her* head and fled the scene, but sadly, in a crisis, her instinct was to freeze. She froze now, inches from this strange man, who looked very sleepy and confused. He shook his head as if to clear it. "Hi!" he said, rather angrily. "You scared me!"

"I'm sorry," Deidre said. She decided not to volunteer anything else.

He gave his head another doglike shake, apparently not convinced he was really awake. He was a nice-looking man, somewhere in his twenties, not classically handsome, but his features had a pleasing overall effect. He was blond, with just enough wave in his hair to keep it perpetually tousled. His eyes, instead of the blue Deidre had expected, were a deep shade of green, which seemed especially intense because he stared right into Deidre's eyes. "Did you lose a contact lens?" he asked, still trying to make sense of the situation.

"No, I . . ." For a terrible second Deidre couldn't think of any explanation. Then God must have taken pity on her, because miraculously, she thought of a story. "I saw a wasp flying around you and I didn't want him to land on you. So I hit him with your magazine."

"Oh." He sat up and lifted the magazine, looking for the wasp. "Oh," he said again. "Well, thank you."

"It probably crawled away to die," Deidre said, determined to appear truthful. "They do that."

"Do they?" He was looking into her eyes again. He had a strange, friendly kind of intensity about him. It reminded Deidre of the look a puppy has when he brings his master a toy. "What's your name?" he asked.

"Deidre," Deidre said, dropping her eyes shyly.

"Deidre!" he said. "That's beautiful!"

The blush was coming back. "Thank you," she choked out. "I really don't like it that much. People usually spell it wrong or pronounce it wrong—"

"My name is Jeff," he interrupted. "Do you live here, Deidre?"

"Yes," she said. "Do you?" It occurred to her suddenly that she knew almost all the tenants but she'd never seen this man. For the first time she felt a little frightened being alone with him.

"Yeah. I just moved in and I don't know anybody yet. Are the people in this building nice?"

"Oh, yes," Deidre said. By now she had the presence of mind to get up from her knees and sit in the deck chair next to his. "Oh! You just moved in? I bet you're in the apartment right above ours. Do you play the piano?"

"Uh-oh!" he said. "That goddamned manager swore to me it wouldn't carry through the walls! That was the first thing I asked him."

"You didn't disturb anyone!" Deidre said quickly. "I thought your playing was very good."

"Are you sure? I mean, you're sure it's okay?"

"Yes. Yesterday you played a song I really liked."

"Well, thanks, but do your mom and dad like music as much as you do?"

"I don't have a father, and my mother is never home until after six."

"Oh, great. I only play in the daytime. I work at night."

"What do you do?"

He looked insulted. "I play the piano!"

"Oh, I'm sorry. I didn't realize you were a professional musician. I thought it was just like a hobby."

"It's my life," he said, very seriously. "It's my whole life."

"Okay," Deidre said. "You mean you go somewhere at night and perform? That's pretty neat."

"Yeah," he agreed. "I play in a small club in Fort Lauderdale. It's a stepping-stone."

"To what?"

"I don't know. A big club in Fort Lauderdale. A big club in Miami. A hit record. Rule the world. Whatever."

"Wow," Deidre said.

"I sing too," he said, clearly warming to the topic. "And I compose a little. I compose classical music. Right now, for instance, I'm working on a rhapsody."

"God. I don't even know what a rhapsody is."

"I didn't, either, until I looked it up. It's a free-form piece that expresses great elation or happiness."

"I'm really impressed," Deidre said. "What's the name of your club?"

His expression suddenly became less friendly. "The *name* of it, you mean?"

"Yeah. Maybe I've heard of it."

He fidgeted. "Aren't you a little young to know the nightclub scene?"

"Yeah, but I grew up in Fort Lauderdale. Is it Yesterday's or Stan's or . . ."

He was rocking back and forth now, as if impatient or irritated. "It's called the Sundowner Lounge."

"I've never heard of that. Where is it?"

The rocking got faster. "It's on Federal Highway. Near the Holiday Inn at Twenty-sixth Street."

"Oh, I know right where you are. But there's no club around there. Next to the Holiday Inn is a pancake house."

"Okay!" he exploded. "It's *inside* the Holiday Inn! So what?"

Deidre drew back. She didn't know why he was angry. "Okay!" she said. "So it's like, a hotel bar."

"*Motel* bar," he said glumly. "*Motel* bar." He sat back in his chair as if he'd suffered a terrible defeat.

Deidre thought he was the moodiest man she'd ever seen. "Is there something wrong with that?" she asked timidly.

"Yeah. There's something wrong with that." He picked at a hangnail. "It's the bottom of the barrel, is what's wrong with it. It's just about one step up from dog shows and fairs." He brought his thumb up to his mouth and bit the hangnail viciously.

Deidre felt strangely responsible for all this. "Well," she said nervously, "at least you aren't playing dog shows and fairs."

He looked up and laughed. "That's true," he said. Then his expression turned serious again. "I won't always be a lounge lizard, though. I know it. You have to start there, but you don't have to finish there. The important thing is where you finish."

"That's right," Deidre said. "I agree."

He lifted his chin, like a little boy. "Someday, you know, maybe even when I'm dead, they'll find my rhapsody and they'll say, 'By God, Jeff Elliot was the greatest musical genius who ever lived!' "

Deidre laughed. "Sure they will."

"Do you want to hear it?"

"What?"

"My thing. My rhapsody. Come on up and I'll play it for you. I've got to finish unpacking anyway. I just came down for a break. You can talk to me while I unpack. And then I'll play my masterpiece for you."

"No! You can't play it now!" Deidre said. "My mom is working in the dining room. You can't play on weekends or she might complain."

"Oh," he said. "Is your mom the grouchy type?"

"Well, no, but I don't want you to get in any trouble."

"What a sweet kid you are!" he said. "I really like you. And you're my first friend in this building. Want to come up anyway? I've really got to get out of the sun because I'm broiling." He actually pulled the waistband of his shorts down a few inches to check for sunburn.

"Oh, no, I'd better not," Deidre stammered, trying

not to look where he was looking. "I mean, no offense or anything, but I don't . . . *know* you."

"Oh!" he said. He looked genuinely hurt. "Jeez, Deidre, I'm not any kind of bad person or anything. I guess they teach you kids that kind of stuff in school nowadays, don't they?"

"Yeah," she said, blushing again.

"Well, I guess that's a good idea," he said. "Sad, though. Well, okay! Maybe some other time when you've known me longer and nobody reports any ax murders in the neighborhood, right? It's an open invitation."

"Thanks," Deidre said, gripping the arms of her chair to keep from jumping up and following him.

He got up and patted her shoulder. "Don't do anything I wouldn't do!" he said, and loped away.

The pool area was very quiet after he left. Like a cemetery, Deidre thought.

3

As usual Susie was late. Deidre was pretty sure the expedition would fail anyway. She'd already walked past Embraceable Zoo and the only person behind the counter was an angry-looking middle-aged woman. Sunday was probably Curt Wyler's day off, when he fooled around with all the junior-high girls he picked up during the week. Deidre secretly hoped by the time Susie got back to him, he'd have lost interest and gone on to another victim. That would really be the best thing all around.

Knowing from experience that Susie wouldn't be along for another half hour, Deidre drifted into Camelot to listen to the music. There was a poster of a heavy metal band on the wall, called Raging Inferno. They all wore flame-patterned tights. Deidre made a careful study of the poster, in the interest of developing her musical education.

"May I help you?"

She turned and almost bumped against a gorgeous blond clerk. Let Curt Wyler top this guy! "I was just . . ." she stammered.

"Were you looking for something in particular?" he asked, oblivious to the reaction he was causing.

"Yeah. I was wondering"—Deidre thought frantically—"where the Billy Joel tapes were."

He frowned, as if surprised that was what she wanted. Then he pointed in a cute, awkward way, back over his shoulder. "Pop and Rock," he said. "Alphabetical by artist."

"Thanks." She hurried away. Of course, once she got there, she didn't know what to look for. She didn't know the name of the song she loved. All she had was her mother's opinion it wasn't "Allentown." She certainly wasn't going to hum anything for that clerk! She took *Billy Joel's Greatest Hits* from the slot. There was probably an even chance the song Jeff had been playing was one of those. The cover showed Billy Joel sitting at a black piano with a spotlight on him. He was a piano player! She supposed she had known that, but hadn't thought about it consciously. Naturally he would be one of Jeff's heroes. She decided she would buy the tape even if it turned out the magical waltzing song wasn't on it. Probably all Billy Joel's songs were important to Jeff. Maybe she would run into him at the pool sometime and they could discuss it. She bought the tape quickly, spending all her money, hurrying through the transaction before she could lose the impulse. She almost ran from the store, her heart racing as if she'd shoplifted something.

Back in the food court she found Susie at a table in the far corner, working on a Häagen-Dazs milk shake. "Where have you been?" she accused. "I've been waiting here forever!"

"I was here first!" Deidre snapped, still unsettled. "You weren't here, so I went shopping."

"What'd you get?" Susie asked, looking at the bag.

Deidre sat down and took a tissue from her purse to clean off the table. "A Billy Joel tape." She felt heat coming into her face.

"Billy Joel!" Susie squeaked. "What did you buy that for?"

Deidre focused all her attention on the cleaning of the table, picking up Susie's milkshake and polishing under it. "What's wrong with Billy Joel? He was one of the greatest artists of the last decade, in case you didn't know."

"I knew!" Susie said. "I just didn't know you *cared.* I never heard you say a word about him before."

"Well, people's taste changes all the time," Deidre said. "I like to be open to new things. That's how you grow."

"Oh." Susie nodded. "I'm glad you told me that."

"I'm not being snotty!" Deidre said.

"Oh, yes, you are! Hey, no problem! If you're suddenly crazy about Billy Joel, if he's helping you *grow,* I think that's great. You want something to eat? They've got rum raisin today." Both girls liked to eat rum-raisin ice-cream and pretend they were getting a buzz.

"No, I'm not hungry. I'm feeling a little funny today."

"Well, good. At least that explains why you're *acting* so funny."

"How's Uncle Jack?" Deidre asked, anxious to change the subject.

"Who cares?" Susie said. She sucked violently at the bottom of her shake, making an embarrassing noise. "Let's get to the good stuff. Are you ready to see a little piece of heaven?"

"He's not there, is he?" Deidre asked, feeling unsettled all over again.

"Sure he's there. I just went by. He didn't see me, though. He's got on one of those Gold's Gym T-shirts. Do you think that means he works out?"

"No. He probably just bought the shirt so people would think that."

"I don't know. He's got a fantastic behind." Susie illustrated with her hands.

Deidre felt strangely trapped and scared. She didn't want to be in this situation. She wanted to go home and listen to her tape. "Just exactly what are we going to do?" she asked.

"Just go over and talk to him. Get to know him. And if he asks me out again . . . well, who knows?" Susie flipped her hair back and smiled the same brassy smile she'd been using since the first grade, when she was showing off missing teeth.

"Are you sure you want me to go with you?"

"Yes! I'd be scared to do this alone!"

"Then how can you think about going out with him? Or am I supposed to go along for that too?"

"Uh-uh, no way. He might have bad taste and start liking you better than me! I just need you right now in the early stages of this thing for moral support. And as a witness. So I can believe this is happening to me."

"I'm having a little trouble believing it myself. Okay, what do we do?"

"Just go over there. It's up to him to make another move. We'll just act like we came in to look at his . . . toys." Susie giggled.

Deidre stood up uncertainly. "Okay." She wished her heart would calm down. It was skipping all over the place.

The first look she got at Curt Wyler was his rear end. He was bending down, trying to fix a little train track that ran around the floor. Deidre revised her opinion and decided maybe he did work out after all.

To get his attention Susie went to a display of Surfing Barbies and said loudly, "What a doll!"

He straightened up and turned around, then laughed softly, not the least embarrassed. He had glossy brown hair and straight black eyebrows that made all his expressions, even his smile, look a little sinister. But he was handsome. Drop-dead, male-model, Hollywood-contract handsome. Why, Deidre wondered, did a great-looking guy like him want to date a girl in junior high? "Hi," he said, hesitating just a second, ". . . Susie."

She turned around. "Oh, hi, Curt. I didn't see you when I first came in. This is my cousin Deidre."

"Hi," he said, soft and syrupy. He looked Deidre up and down shamelessly. His eyes were an odd shade of brown, almost reddish, like strongly brewed tea.

"Hi," Deidre murmured, looking away. It seemed all she was going to do today was blush and have heart palpitations.

Curt leaned back against the sales counter, hooking his thumbs in his belt loops. "Aren't you kind of a big girl to be playing with dolls?" he asked Susie.

"Depends on what kind." She smiled.

Deidre understood the attraction now. Susie had always been a compulsive flirt, but her talents were wasted at Ramblewood Junior High, where boys deflected innuendos and double entendres with a terse "Shut up, will you?" Now Susie had found her male counterpart, a world-class flirt worthy of her abilities. They could practice their routines on each other, perfect their craft, steal ideas.

"You been thinking about what I said?" Curt asked in that same silken voice. From his manner you'd think he'd offered Susie the Taj Mahal or something, instead of just an evening of *his* company. Deidre decided she didn't like this guy at all. She wondered how easy it would be to scare Susie away from him.

Susie smiled crookedly. "Well, I don't know. Where do you want to take me?"

He laughed softly again. "Well . . ."

Just then the middle-aged lady appeared from the stock room, holding a plastic AK-47. "Curt!" she said, in a voice like a grackle's. "Did you count these machine guns yet?"

His body immediately changed from a languid S-curve to a stiff capital I. "I don't know, Mrs. McKenzie," he said nervously. "Is there a tag on them?"

"I certainly don't see one!"

"Well," he said, "I guess I was going to do those after lunch."

She consulted her watch. "There's plenty of time *now*," she said. She looked at the girls pointedly. "Unless you're ringing up a *sale*."

Curt was breathing shallowly, like a little boy afraid of getting a spanking. "This young lady"—he gestured toward Susie—"was just having trouble making up her mind."

The woman looked cynically at Susie. "Well, take care of her and then come on back. I'm not doing this whole damn inventory alone!"

"Right. You got it." Curt smiled weakly. He watched until she was gone. "Bitch!" he added under his breath. His body loosened and settled back against the counter again. "She's the manager," he explained to the girls. "She's really got it in for me. But I have to take it because I've been fired from six different jobs this year and if it happens one more time, my dad will kill me. So, I'd better get back to the stupid inventory. How about it, Susie? Are we on?" He offered up a dazzling smile.

Susie was fondling a stuffed bear, pretending to think, making him wait. "Okay." She smiled, looking at him sideways. "I don't see why not."

"When?" he asked, all business now.

"Next Friday?"

"Perfect. That's when I get paid, if Mrs. McKenzie doesn't lynch me before then."

"Where are we going to go?"

He stretched and yawned. "Oh, let's just keep it loose. Play it by ear."

"Okay."

The grackle-voice pealed out of the depths. "Curt!"

"Yes, ma'am!" he called back. "Jesus. Okay, how do I find your house?"

Deidre shifted her weight impatiently while Susie wrote out the address and phone number. She felt like a Peeping Tom watching all this. What was she doing here, anyway?

Susie offered the piece of paper, then snatched it back when Curt reached for it.

He folded his arms, smiling. "You're a little tease, aren't you?" he said. "That's okay. I can handle *that*."

She went over and pushed the paper gently into his hip pocket. "What should I wear?" she asked.

"As little as possible."

"Curt!" croaked the grackle-woman.

"Coming!" he snapped. "Jesus! Okay. See you Friday, Susie." He turned his hot gaze once more to Deidre. "Nice meeting *you*," he said.

"Same here," Deidre said, affecting boredom.

Mrs. McKenzie roared out of the stockroom, grabbed Curt by the arm, and hauled him away. "Honest, Mrs. McKenzie, I was on my way. . . ." he pleaded as she yanked him behind the curtains.

Susie took a deep breath and let it out. "Well?" she asked Deidre.

"Well, what?" Deidre said. She gestured for them to walk away if they were going to talk about Curt.

"What did you think?" Susie asked as they merged into mall traffic. "Is he the most gorgeous thing you've ever seen?"

Deidre had never felt more confused in her life. "He's *one* of the most gorgeous things I've ever seen," she said slowly. "But . . . I really don't think you should go out with him."

Susie stopped walking. "Why?"

Deidre stopped walking. "Well. Because. I mean, you don't have all that much experience, you know? And I think it's obvious, he *does*."

"Well, naturally! He's two years older than me. Anyway, I like the idea he's had some experience. He can . . . teach me things."

"Susie!"

"What?"

Deidre gestured impotently. "Don't you think you're

headed for some kind of disaster here? He's a very big boy!"

"He sure is!" Susie said happily.

"Susie, what's he going to expect from you? Especially the way you act with him! You can see what kind of a guy he is!"

"Yes!" Susie said. "I agree. You think I don't know that? That's what I like about him. I'm so sick of the little boys in our school, I could scream. I really don't think you get it, Dee. I'm *trying* to have a little adventure here. That's what I want."

"Well, I think a guy like that would give you more adventure than you can handle."

"How do you know what *I* can handle? Look, just because you're a prude . . ."

"I am not!"

"You are too. And you know what else? You're jealous!"

"You're crazy!" Deidre shouted. Then she forced herself to be calm and rational. This was too important not to treat seriously. "Susie, I'm not. I'm really not. I'm just concerned about you."

"Hey, I understand," Susie said. "You wouldn't have the nerve to do something like this, so now you want to wreck it for me. Well, it won't work. I know what I want and I know what I'm ready for and I am definitely ready for this guy. And if you want to stay a little kid forever, that's your problem. The rest of us want to grow up."

Deidre was so enraged, she couldn't even shout. Her

voice came out like a hoarse whisper. "All I was doing was trying to be your friend. But if you want to ruin your life, go ahead. I just don't want to hear about it when it happens. All right?"

Susie folded her arms. "Fine by me."

There was a moment of hesitation while each of them considered giving in and calling a truce. But the moment went on too long and Deidre turned and began walking toward the exits.

"Get a life!" Susie shouted after her.

I

Before she went to bed that night, Deidre played the cassette. She decided to use the headphones. She didn't want her mother to hear the songs and come in and start reminiscing about the last ten years.

She loved the tape from the first minute. She had always been vaguely aware of how Billy Joel sounded, but she had never really listened to his lyrics before. He was a storyteller. He told complicated stories; the man who didn't want his girlfriend to change, the guy who wanted to live his own life, the soldier, the factory worker, the poor boy in love with the rich girl. They all seemed like real people. Deidre liked Jeff all the more, knowing he had such good taste.

Then the crazy, glorious happy waltz came on. As soon as the opening chords sounded, she recognized it and stopped the tape and consulted the cassette. The title was "Piano Man." She started the tape again and listened to the lyrics carefully.

It was nothing like what she'd expected. The melody had made her feel so happy, she'd been expecting an upbeat song, a celebration of something. But this song was very, very sad. It was about a guy who played piano in a bar, just like Jeff. Just like Jeff, he was really talented, but couldn't get a big break. In fact, the whole bar was full of people who hadn't realized their dreams. It was the saddest, bravest, most wistful story Deidre had ever heard. She played the tape over and over, slowly pulling a pillow into her arms and cradling it, brushing away tears with the back of her hand.

Finally, she pushed the stop button and just listened to the silence. She took off the headphones. She understood Jeff Elliot now. She really knew who he was. He was a tragic hero, trying to beat odds that couldn't be beaten. Inside he was very, very lonely. Probably most people didn't understand him. But she knew that she did.

That, she told herself, was what love was *really* about. Susie, who thought she was so grown up and sophisticated, didn't have a clue. Susie thought love was when you found someone who wanted to jump on you as much as you wanted to jump on him.

But real love was like this moment. When you could see clearly into another person's heart and understand him. Although she'd only met him once, Deidre knew she loved Jeff Elliot as much as anyone else ever could.

Even though he would probably never know.

Slowly, gently, she pushed the pillow aside and stood up. She put the cassette away in its case and got ready for bed. On an impulse she put on her best nightgown, the one her mother had brought back from New York last Christmas. It was white, with a pattern of tiny lilac bunches, trimmed with lilac ribbons. She brushed her hair until it glowed and crackled in the lamplight.

She turned down the bed and placed the extra pillow vertically, so it was like another person lying there. She lay down next to it, barely touching, letting it rest gently against her back. She imagined the pillow yawning comfortably and putting an invisible arm around her waist.

And just as she was falling asleep, when her mind hovered in a rich twilight between reality and dreams, she felt the pillow pull her close and whisper a sad little lullaby written just for her.

4

Deidre trudged home in the blinding, shimmering heat. All day in school Susie had ignored her, which would have been okay except Susie made a *show* of ignoring her, always timing herself to cross Deidre's path so she could stick her nose in the air. Deidre didn't care that much. They had gone through this routine about a thousand times before, but it was a minor annoyance, like a headache or an ingrown toenail, that added to the burdens of the day. The air conditioning at school was broken, too, so kids were sweltering through their classes. Boys kept trying to unbutton or remove shirts until they were reprimanded for it. Girls wore their hair in lopsided twists and tails. Everyone looked sapped. Teachers foolishly kept trying to teach things, even though with four days to go, nobody's heart was really in it.

Three more blocks. Deidre pictured her refrigerator. Not just because it was cold, but because she loved the refrigerator. It was her power source, the place she stored her creative energy. When she couldn't sleep at night, she would picture the contents of the refrigerator and imagine using the ingredients in various combinations. She loved the day after grocery shopping, when the refrigerator was full and the possibilities endless.

She always made a special dinner for her mother on Monday. It gave them both something to look forward to on the most difficult day of the week.

Today, the theme would have to be *cold.* There were a lot of salad vegetables in the hydrator—tomatoes and celery and peppers. There was ham and Swiss cheese. She could make a chef salad and mix up some kind of wonderful dressing with the leftover sour cream—no, that was too obvious. She could put the sour cream and the vegetables together and make gazpacho! That would be fun! She would flavor it with garlic and a little Tabasco and serve the ham cold on the side. Any good bread? Yes! Half a loaf of French, from Saturday's spaghetti. Iced coffee. Peach ice cream. The world was a cool, wonderful place again.

She let herself into the apartment and kicked up the air conditioning. Her mom always left the place too hot. She went immediately to the refrigerator and found a Post-It note. *Have to work very late. Eat without me. Sorry. Bye.*

Deidre crumpled the note and threw it on the floor. She felt too heavy and tired to move. She put her arms around the refrigerator and rested her forehead against it, listening to the hum. Then she looked inside, listlessly, to see if there was anything she wanted. But the idea of food made her almost sick. She decided she would just have a bowl of cereal later and eat a Milky Way from the freezer.

Deidre went to her room and changed, kicking her clothes into a corner and putting on shorts and her favorite, most comforting T-shirt, the faded, oversized pink one. Then she flopped across her bed and listened to silence. The moment her body relaxed a wave of self-pity rolled up and came out as a little sob. Deidre was surprised, but once she started it felt good and she just let it happen. Hot, loose tears streamed down her face.

She fed the feeling with her thoughts. Everyone had abandoned her. Her mother only cared about work. Susie hated her. Her father was dead. . . . She eagerly thought of everything she could to sustain the momentum of her crying. Aunt Carol and Uncle Jack's divorce. The time she missed the finals of the National Spelling Bee. Her grandfather's funeral three years ago. It felt wonderful, like a purge, pulling the tension from her body and leaving her light and clean and pleasantly exhausted.

She was almost asleep when she heard the music. It was Jeff upstairs playing "I Wish It Would Rain." His technique was beautiful. Every note was shimmery and elusive, piercing the air like a delicate knife. Deidre let the music carry her up into a kind of suspension where nothing mattered. She felt like a spiderweb full of raindrops.

She thought about Jeff himself. She could remember their whole conversation by the pool. She wondered if he really meant it when he'd invited her up. He seemed like the type of guy who just said things—*Let's get together, call me sometime*—then forgot all about it. He was just nice to everyone. She could still remember the shock of looking into those intense green eyes. *Deidre,* he'd said, *what a beautiful name! What a sweet kid you are! I really like you.* It all came back, word for word, like an ice cream flavor she'd forgotten and rediscovered.

Slowly, not really deciding yet, she got up and stood in front of the mirror. Her face was red and swollen from crying. She picked up her brush and worked on her hair, marking time. There was a brief silence upstairs, then he played "Higher Love." It was a sign.

She splashed her face with cold water. The swelling was almost gone, leaving her a little flushed. Prettier, really, than makeup could have done. *You're my first friend in this building.* He had said it. He had claimed her as a friend. *It's an open invitation.*

Deidre knew she had nothing to lose except an evening alone in an empty apartment. She put on some pale pink lipstick, splashed her wrists and throat with Muguet des Bois, and followed the music upstairs.

By the time she got to his door, the song had changed to "Words Get in the Way." One of Deidre's favorites.

The omens were coming thick and fast. She knocked loudly, so he could hear her over the music. It stopped immediately and footsteps came toward the door. For some reason Deidre's heart was beating very fast. She had a silly urge to run, but fought it down.

He opened the door and looked at Deidre with mild bewilderment. Today he wore aqua shorts and a tropical shirt printed with hummingbirds and hibiscus. His feet were bare. He frowned at Deidre for just a second and then a radiant smile broke out. "Oh! It's you. From the pool. *Deidre.* The girl with the beautiful name. Was I playing too loud?"

Deidre was blushing from the compliment to her name. "No," she said. "I just . . ." *What? I just came up hoping to be friends with you?*

"Well, come on in!" he said, standing aside. "Don't *look* at anything, though, because this place is still a mess. I keep unpacking, but it doesn't get any neater in here."

She followed him into the shadowy hallway. Architecturally, his apartment was identical to hers. But there the resemblance ended. Deidre thought she had never seen a messier, more chaotic environment in her life. The hall was stacked with rows and rows of empty moving boxes. What small aisle was left was filled up with a ten-speed, a cat's litter box, and a huge stack of magazines, which looked about to topple.

Following him up the hall, she glimpsed a kitchen with every inch of counter space full of objects, grocery sacks, and more boxes. On the floor near the laundry closet was a mountain of colorful clothing and a music rack with a dinner jacket hanging on it.

But the living room was the worst. It was crowded with furniture: couch, chairs, the piano, an electronic keyboard, TV, VCR, a child's rocking horse, an expensive-looking mirrored bar unit, and a big antique desk. There were more boxes in here, full of books, videotapes (Deidre noticed in particular *Attack of the Killer Tomatoes*), sheet music, office supplies, and cat toys. There were also used champagne glasses on windowsills and end tables, and a newspaper, whose sections were blowing around under the ceiling fan, giving the effect of tumbleweeds. Deidre tried very hard not to look at a pair of briefs, Mediterranean blue with white piping, which lay on the floor by the couch. She tried even harder not to imagine how they'd got there.

Luckily, she was diverted from this line of thought because she had come close to the piano and realized she was inches from a huge tawny tomcat who was glowering at her. "Oh!" she cried involuntarily.

Jeff, who was excavating the couch so she could sit down, glanced up to see what was wrong. "That's the cat," he explained.

"Yes, I know," Deidre said, trying not to be unnerved by the animal's baleful stare. "I just . . . didn't realize he was alive."

Jeff came over to the piano and scrutinized the cat. "Sometimes it's hard to tell with him," he said. He

44

picked up one of the cat's hind legs and pump-handled it. The cat kicked him off indignantly. "Yep. He's alive. Sit down, Deidre. Can I get you something? What do I have that a kid could drink? I know! How about pineapple juice?"

It wouldn't be Deidre's first choice, but since he offered nothing else, she said, "Sure."

"Great!" He went to the kitchen and made a noise like pots and pans falling down a stairway. "Whoops!" he said to himself.

While he worked, Deidre snooped. She pulled over a box marked ART OBJECTS. In the top was a plastic shower curtain made to look like piano keys. Beneath that was one of those plastic flowers that dance to radio music. Deidre found a poster and unrolled it.

"Are you out of school now?" he called over the sound of glass breaking.

It was a travel poster of Paris, the Eiffel Tower with a big spray of wisteria in the foreground. "Do you mean for this year?" Deidre asked. She hoped he meant she could pass for a senior.

There was a loud *clunk*. "Jeez!" he commented. "Yeah. I don't even know what month it is anymore. Is it summer?"

"Almost," she said, rolling the poster up carefully so he wouldn't suspect anything. The cat glared with disapproval. "We still have to finish this week. Then it's summer." In the bottom of the box were three eight-by-ten photographs, all in identical brass frames. Jimmy

Buffett, the cat, and a girl in an orange bikini, washing a car.

"Here's to summer," he said, carrying in two champagne flutes of pineapple juice. A bag of Oreos swung from between his teeth.

"Thanks," Deidre said, taking the glass. "Fancy!" she commented.

"Fancy is all I have." He laughed. "I have twenty-four of these. Well. Twenty-three now. It's good stuff, full lead crystal. My mom gave them to me years ago. All I have is them and a set of bone-china dessert dishes. I was thinking when I first moved in here I should get some coffee cups or plates or something, but you know, it's kind of fun using the good stuff all the time."

"Yeah, I see what you mean. You mean you drink your coffee out of these?"

"Yeah." He smiled as if the memory of it pleased him. "So how do you like my place?"

Deidre was trying to think of a polite euphemism when she realized he was joking. "I can't see how you live like this! If it was me, I would have unpacked everything and put it all away the first day."

He tore the Oreo bag open down the wrong side and offered it to Deidre. "Things like that don't bother me. Nothing bothers me except *people.*"

She wished he'd elaborate but he didn't. "One of the things I came up to tell you was that I really like the way you do 'Piano Man.' You were practicing it Friday and it sounded just beautiful."

He paused, holding a cookie in front of his mouth. "You like that song?" His eyes glowed, almost. They were not a cool green at all, but the warm green of rivers.

"Oh, yes!" Deidre said, trying to sound as if she hadn't heard the song for the first time yesterday. "I love it."

"I put it in all my shows," he said reverently. "It means a lot to me. I feel like Billy Joel wrote it for all us guys who . . . might or might not make it. When he wrote it he was looking back, you know? Everyone has dreams. But just a few people actually make them come true. And I'm damned if I'm going to let anything keep me from being one of those people! That's what the song's about. Just because you're struggling or you look like a fool . . . it doesn't mean tomorrow you won't coast up on a big wave"—the cookie hand arched up gracefully—"just like he did. Do you know my favorite line from that song?"

Deidre was a little breathless from this speech. "No."

" 'Man, what are you doing here?' That's what I ask myself every night in that stupid bar, playing for people who don't listen, getting applause from three people. Do you know what three people applauding *sounds* like? It's a lot worse than dead silence, let me tell you. The other night I had just finished a ballad and some guy retched all over the floor. The customers looked at him, instead of me. They thought his show was better than mine. But when I get down, Deidre, I say, 'Man, what are *you* doing here?' That's the main thing. I'm going where I belong *someday*."

"Sure you are," Deidre said passionately. "You're really good."

"I *am*," he agreed, chugging his pineapple juice. "I know I am. But you know what? So is everybody else. That's the thing I didn't figure on. So is everybody else. . . ." His eyes unfocused a second, then he stood up and went to the piano. "Want to hear part of a masterpiece?" he asked.

"Your rhapsody?" Deidre asked. "Yes, I'd love to hear it."

"Smart answer." He grinned. "Any other answer and you don't get invited back." He sat on the bench, tugging it into place with a familiar jerk, like something he had done a million times before. The cat, apparently knowing what to expect, sat up and looked attentive. "All right—literally, here goes nothing! This is Untitled Rhapsody Number One by Jeff Elliot." He clownishly suspended his fingers high above the keys and let them drop. But then the clowning stopped.

There was suddenly a different man at the piano, a man Deidre didn't know. His back was straight and formal, his eyes half closed, as if he were listening to something in the distance. A faint swaying of the shoulders expanded into fierce, measured strokes of arms, wrists, fingers.

Slowly and elegantly, his work at the keys built a structure of sound in the air, crystal filaments twisted and fused into bridges, towers, castles, a chandelier full of prisms, a scrap of cloud in a windstorm, a flurry of birds, a shiver. A kiss . . .

Then abruptly it stopped. Deidre toppled and slid down into the silence, grieving for the moment just past when the last chord was still poised in the air. She had forgotten the rhapsody was unfinished. She swallowed and tried to catch her breath.

The cat closed his eyes and went back to sleep. Jeff turned around. "Well?"

Deidre realized she had not expected him to be good. Maybe a good musician, but not a composer. Someone who worked in a bar shouldn't be able to write music like that. Everyone who was talented should be famous. Otherwise it would be—it was—a terrible tragedy.

"It's the most beautiful thing I've ever heard," she said softly.

He smiled. "You're easy," he chided. "I wish I could find the title. Then I think I could get enough of a focus to finish it. I think I want to call it something French, you know? The music makes me think of Paris."

"Did you live there?" Deidre cried eagerly, thinking of the poster.

He came and sat down in his place. "Live there? I've never even visited. What would make you think that?"

"Oh," she said. She looked down, blushing. "I'm sorry. I saw your . . . while you were in the kitchen, I sort of glanced through that box and I saw you had a poster and—"

"*That* box?" he interrupted. He didn't look pleased.

"Yes," Deidre said. "I'm really sorry. I'm kind of . . . a *curious* person."

"That's a good word for it," he said. "My mom used to say I was *imaginative.* That meant I was a liar."

Deidre laughed, realizing he had already forgiven her. "If you've never been to Paris, why do you have a poster for it?"

"Oh. Well. I like the feeling of Paris, you know? I know I would like it, if I went. I just know. Paris has got something to do with . . . me."

Strangely, Deidre knew just what he meant. There were things like that for her too. In fact, she now realized, Jeff had been like that. She had just *known* they could be friends.

Meanwhile, he was blushing. "Did you look at *all* the stuff in that box?"

She lowered her eyes. "Yes."

He coughed. "That's my ex."

"Jimmy Buffett?" she asked, to make him laugh.

He grinned. "The lady with the hose. Christine." Then in a different tone he added, "Chrissie."

"Ex-*wife*?" Deidre asked, unable to control herself.

"No. But we lived together two years. I was *trying* to marry her. I asked her all the time."

Deidre couldn't believe he was volunteering so much. Usually you couldn't get an adult to tell you anything. It was a rare opportunity for a "curious" person like Deidre, and she meant to exploit it for all it was worth. "She said no?"

He smiled bitterly. "Always. She didn't like my career. She wanted me to get a regular job and just play as a hobby. She thought I was driving myself crazy wishing for something that would never happen. But see? If I did that, it *would* kill me. I can do anything except give up. If I don't have some kind of big thing to hope for, I'm dead."

"Sure," said Deidre. She decided she hated Chrissie. "So if you broke up with her, why do you still have the picture?"

He grinned, lopsided. "If I don't have some kind of big thing to hope for, I'm dead."

"You want her back?"

"Sure. You know. It was a habit." His attempt to look casual was pathetic.

Something about him made Deidre feel very bold. "Well, she's very pretty. But obviously she didn't understand you. So you know, that's not my idea of love."

He was watching her raptly, as if her opinion really mattered. "Yeah. True. Maybe. I don't know. But I miss her. If I hadn't gotten custody of Cyril, I don't know what I'd have done."

Deidre breathed in sharply. She looked at the rocking horse. "You guys had a baby?"

Jeff exploded with laughter. He pointed to the piano, where the cat had just hoisted its leg to take a bath. "*That's* Cyril!" he explained.

I

It was after ten when her mother finally came home. Deidre was in her room, listening to Billy Joel. Normally, she would have gone out to greet her mother, but tonight she felt like staying where she was and letting her mother look for her.

Mrs. Holland swished into the bedroom, wearing a flowered sundress and little pearl earrings. Her hair was up. "Hi!" she said.

"Hi," Deidre said.

She was wearing more lipstick than usual too. "Turn that down, sweetie, it's too loud."

Deidre stopped the tape.

"How was your evening?" her mother asked, sitting on the bed.

"Fine. How was *yours*?"

"Awful. We're so backed up. You'd think this would be the slow season, but it's not. Suddenly everyone wants a financial makeover."

"How's Mr. Maxwell?"

"I don't know. I don't think he handles stress well. He keeps everything inside."

"I've never seen you wear that dress to work before."

"I know. It was so *hot*. I decided, what the hell?"

"Yeah. What the hell?"

"Did you have something to eat?"

"I managed."

"We had the worst sandwiches in the world. I'm still hungry. Is there anything good in the refrigerator?"

"I can't remember," Deidre said, turning the tape back on. "You'll have to go see for yourself."

5

Deidre lifted the lid on the pot roast for the twenty-seventh time, trying not to listen to a fresh burst of giggling from the living room. She realized she'd made a terrible error, choosing an entrée that could be left to simmer on the stove. She had no excuse not to go in and talk to them.

She fanned the steam from the pot toward her face and inhaled deeply, allowing the aromas to envelop and comfort her: a luxurious brown-gravy smell, enriched with burgundy, punctuated by carrots and onions, seasoned with parsley and thyme and Deidre's secret weapon, a handful of fresh mint. A few months ago she'd discovered mint could be substituted for bay leaf in simmered dishes, with spectacular results. It was all too good for Mr. Maxwell, she thought. What had he done to deserve such riches?

More laughter. Deidre's mother seemed to think Mr. Maxwell was a stand-up comedian. Deidre checked the melon slices in the refrigerator and the biscuits in the warming oven. Nothing required her attention. She sighed and went into the living room.

They were sitting side by side on the couch, like a couple of puppies. Mr. Maxwell was small, almost delicately built, with fair hair and weirdly deep-set blue eyes, accented by schoolboy horn-rims. He wore an expensive-looking suit, a Movado watch, and a shirt with French cuffs. Also a ring with a black background and some insignia Deidre didn't understand, a letter *G* surrounded by carpentry tools. She could smell his cologne all the way across the room. It was like wild cherry cough syrup. Deidre felt uneasy the moment she met him, unable to decide if she found him attractive or repulsive.

"Here's the chef!" he greeted Deidre with the false gaiety of someone who expects to be hated. "I hope you aren't going to too much trouble, Deidre."

"Cooking comes naturally to her," said her mother. "It's almost like a gift."

"It is a gift!" he said emphatically. "Of course it is. As far as I'm concerned it's the same as being able to paint or write poetry or anything like that."

"I think so too," Deidre said shyly. "I'd like to get into the CIA someday."

Mr. Maxwell blinked. "You lost me."

"The Culinary Institute of America," Deidre's mother explained. "It's a cooking school."

"It's more than a cooking school!" Deidre said. "It turns out the best chefs in the country."

"Would you like to own your own restaurant?" Mr. Maxwell asked.

"Yes." She thought of Jeff suddenly. "Or a nightclub."

"Oh, I think that's fascinating!" he said sincerely. "I think cooking would be a wonderful talent to have. Because everyone appreciates it so much."

"That's true," Deidre said. "But it's also kind of sad. You can't do anything that lasts. Everything you make gets destroyed."

"I hadn't thought of that," he agreed. "My God! Think where all your work actually ends up!"

"Henry!" Deidre's mother cried, slapping at him. "You're terrible!"

Deidre's stomach twisted. She was confused. She was beginning to like Mr. Maxwell, but she didn't like the idea of him with her mother. They looked strange together. He was so small and neat and intellectual. He made her mother look too tall and showy beside him. Mrs. Holland was wearing another one of the new dresses she'd bought since she started this job, a blue sleeveless number with a full skirt, like something from the 1950s. That was it, Deidre thought. She *didn't* dislike Mr. Maxwell. She disliked her mother *around* Mr. Maxwell.

"I think dinner's ready," Deidre said standing up.

"Very intelligent," she heard Mr. Maxwell murmur as she left the room.

"Do you think so?" Mrs. Holland asked him, as if he were a child-development specialist. As if she, the mother, had never noticed this.

Deidre rattled a few pots and pans so she couldn't hear any more. She really wanted to get through this evening without getting too upset.

∎

"Tell Mr. Maxwell about your grades," Mrs. Holland said, during the melon.

Again Deidre felt rattled. It was like *Sing something for your aunt Betty.* "Today was the last day of school," Deidre said. "So we got our grades."

Mr. Maxwell waited politely for more, then laughed a little. "How *were* your grades?"

"A's," Deidre said, keeping her eyes on her plate.

"How *many* A's?" her mother prompted.

"*All* A's," Deidre said grumpily.

Mrs. Holland turned to Mr. Maxwell. "Straight A's. She had a four-point average this semester."

"That's wonderful," Mr. Maxwell said discreetly, as if sensing her discomfort. "What grade will you be in next year?"

"Ninth. Next year I start high school."

"High school." He shuddered. "What a horrible thought!"

"Don't say that!" Mrs. Holland cried. She turned to Deidre. "*My* high school years were the happiest of my life."

"Mine were like a little four-year sample of damnation," said Mr. Maxwell. "On graduation day I got on my knees and thanked God it was finally over."

"Don't *say* things like that to her!" Mrs. Holland said, with real anger. "You'll make her worry!"

"She's not a jellyfish," Mr. Maxwell retorted. "She's smart enough to hear different opinions and make up her own mind. I'm just saying some people go through hell in high school. If she knows that in advance, she won't feel isolated if it happens to her."

"Well," said Deidre's mother, fussing with her napkin, "I think you can bring a lot of trouble on yourself by dwelling on the negatives."

"And I think you can deal with life better if you look it squarely in the eye!"

They glared at each other for several seconds. Then Deidre's mother turned to her with a forced smile. "This melon is really good. What did you do to it?"

"You don't do anything to melon," Deidre said. "You just cut it up." She was strangely excited by this argument. It had never occurred to her that something might be wrong with her mother's boundless optimism. She had always felt guilty for not being able to match it.

The telephone rang. Deidre excused herself and went into the kitchen, balancing the receiver on her shoulder while she checked the roast. "Hello?"

"Dee-Dee, don't hang up on me." It was Susie. They hadn't spoken since the mall incident.

"Hello, Susan," Deidre said grandly.

"Can you talk?"

"As a matter of fact, no. I'm in the middle of a dinner party."

"Oh, sure!"

"I am! There's a lot going on in my life you don't know about. Since you spend all your time hanging around toy stores . . ."

"Dee, please. I haven't got time for that."

"I haven't got time for any of this. I have a roast to carve."

"Just talk to me for two minutes until I calm down."

"What's the matter with you?"

"Don't you remember? It's *tonight*. Curt is picking me up in less than a half hour!"

"Well, what are you upset about? This is what you wanted."

"I know, I know, but . . . I'm just tense. I've never done this before. I wish we hadn't had that stupid fight. If I'd had you to talk to all week, I'd be calm."

"Ha. The only time you're calm is when you're unconscious. Look, I'm not mad, but I really can't talk now. Call me when you get back and tell me everything."

"Just ten more seconds, please. I'm a wreck."

"You got that right. Hey, did you tell Aunt Carol about all this?"

"You can't be serious. You think she'd let me go out with somebody Curt's age?"

"So what are you doing?"

"He's going to pick me up on the corner."

"Just like a whore!"

"Stop it. She thinks I'm with you. Hey! I'm glad I thought of that. In case she calls or anything, just say I'm in the bathroom."

"Okay, but don't cross me up. Don't stay out late or anything!"

"I won't. I told Curt."

"Suze, you have to tell her."

"I know. I will eventually. I just have to time it right."

"I've got to go."

"Could we get together tomorrow at the mall or something?"

"Sure. I want to know you survived your date. And I've got something to tell you."

"What?"

Deidre took a breath. "I think I might be in love."

Now it was real. She had told someone.

"What?"

"I've got to go. Bye." Deidre hung up immediately and busied herself with the food, pushing the phone call out of her mind. She had enough to worry about. For instance, the sharp whispered exchange in the dining room:

"Until you've had kids of your own, keep your theories to yourself!"

"Gladly!"

"Dinner is served!" Deidre interrupted loudly, carrying in the meat and vegetables.

Mr. Maxwell, who had his head down like a scolded child, looked up. "That is just beautiful!" he said.

There was a long interval of three-way silence, biscuit buttering, sipping, cutting, and tasting. Deidre's mother, who never lost her temper, seemed angry out of all proportion to what had happened. Her mouth was set in an angry line.

"This . . ." Mr. Maxwell faltered, glancing at her anxiously, then looking at Deidre. "Everything is just perfect."

"Thank you," she said, knowing it was true.

Mrs. Holland looked up abruptly. "Was your wife a good cook, Henry?"

He laughed. "Gina? No, I wouldn't say that. She could toast bread and heat up spaghetti sauce, but that was about it. We ate out quite a bit."

"That's about like me," Mrs. Holland said, seeming to relax.

"So you see, Deidre, you have a rare talent," said Mr. Maxwell. "Your husband will be thrilled with you."

Deidre smiled to herself, picturing Jeff sitting down to a breakfast she had cooked. The orange juice was in champagne glasses.

"Have you got a boyfriend?" Mr. Maxwell asked, perhaps noticing the smile.

"Deidre's only fourteen," her mother said quickly.

"So?" he asked, then realized he'd stepped on the same thin ice as before. "Oh," he amended.

"Deidre's not the boy-crazy type anyway," her mother said. "She's much too sensible."

Mr. Maxwell glanced at Deidre and raised his eyebrows as if to say, *Bullshit, right?*

To her horror Deidre found herself smiling in agreement. Then she immediately felt guilty for siding with this stranger against her own mother.

Mrs. Holland had been studying her plate again. She looked up. "Tell Deidre about your *orchids,* Henry," she said. Her smile reminded Deidre of something. It was an illustration in one of her old picture books, *Miles of Crocodiles.* It was the same smile one of the crocodiles gave to a stork he was planning to eat.

After the chocolate-raspberry torte Mr. Maxwell said he had to go. Deidre's mother offered to walk him to his car. Deidre fidgeted with dishes for a while, but they were out there such a long time, it drove her crazy. Finally, her "curious" nature got the best of her. She went to the front window and very carefully pulled the curtain aside. They were leaning up against Mr. Maxwell's Fiat, kissing. He had his arms around Deidre's mother and her skirt was all crushed up against the car. It wasn't exactly what Deidre would call a casual kiss. Mr. Maxwell was standing on tiptoe. Deidre felt the weirdest mixture of excitement and revulsion. For a second it was thrilling, like getting a glimpse of something pornographic, then that lurching feeling hit her stomach again. She moved quickly from the window, not even caring how she let the curtain fall, and sat down on the couch, trying to breathe normally. After a second the Fiat revved up and drove away and Mrs. Holland came through the door with a weird look on her face. Deidre felt embarrassed, as if her mom had caught her doing something, instead of the other way around. "Do you want some coffee?" she asked, eager for something to do.

"No, thanks." Mrs. Holland sort of drifted onto a couch. "What did you think of him?"

"I like him."

"You can tell the truth." Her mother smiled.

"I am. I didn't think I was going to like him, but I did."

"He's kind of . . . some people don't like him."

"Well," Deidre said, "he's . . . sort of blunt, but I think he's very smart and funny."

"He's nothing like your father."

Deidre pictured the big, strapping police officer in the photograph on her mother's dresser. "That's true."

Mrs. Holland toyed with her hair. "I've read some books that say you shouldn't talk about your . . . love life to your kids. They say it upsets them."

"Forget it, Mom. What do you want to say?"

"When I walked him out to his car tonight, he kissed me."

"Really?"

"Really."

"I think that's great, Mom. I really do."

"Do you?"

"Yes! Do *you*?"

"I . . . what do you mean?"

"Well, Mom, honestly . . . it doesn't seem like . . . I didn't get the feeling you were all that crazy about him."

"Really?"

"Really."

"I—I don't know. He's . . . not a thing like your father."

"You said that."

"But *you* liked him?"

"Yes. I did."

"I guess I need time to get used to all this," Mrs. Holland said. "I've been out of it too long."

"Is he a good kisser?"

Mrs. Holland smiled. "As a matter of fact, he is."

Deidre had a sudden impulse to tell her mother about Jeff. Then she changed her mind. She just knew somehow it wouldn't work the other way around. "I'm really tired, Mom," she said. "I'm going to bed."

"Good night, sweetie," said her mother, kissing her on the cheek. "I'm glad you like him, anyway. That's one thing I don't have to worry about."

■

Deidre turned out the light and got into bed, but she couldn't sleep. There was so much to think about, and the moon was shining right in the window, making a pinkish glow on everything. She felt embarrassed about what she'd said to Susie. She'd never really admitted to herself that she was in love with Jeff, let alone to someone else. Anyway, it wasn't love, exactly. That would be stupid. After all, the odds of anything really happening with him were pretty slim. She turned impatiently on her other side, trying to block the moonlight out, but now she could see the moon reflected in her mirror and that was even worse. It was almost full, so bright, it was keeping the birds outside awake. The clouds had tinted it a bright, phosphorescent pink, like Cherry 7-Up.

She flipped on her back. Suddenly, she realized for the first time, his bedroom would be right above hers. The floor plans were the same and Deidre had the master bedroom because her furniture was bigger than her mother's. Was he in bed above her right now? She sat up and looked at the clock. No. He was probably still at work. But sometime, during the night, while Deidre was asleep, he would come in and lie down, suspended above her like the other half of an equal sign. All this time they had been sleeping parallel and she hadn't realized. A wonderful peace came over her, imagining this. She saw the two of them in a kind of suspended animation together, like cryogenic experiments, with no floors or ceilings or furniture between them, just darkness and silence. Her mind began to relax and unravel. The glow of the moon was soft, the cries of the mockingbirds rhythmic and hypnotic. . . .

Joyce Sweeney

It was a light, airy apartment with lots of blond wood and pale, textured neutrals. Here and there, a splash of primary color: the poster of Paris, the throw pillows she'd forced him to buy, the flowers she'd brought with the groceries and arranged in the old champagne bottle he used for a vase.

Jeff padded down the hallway, his hair dripping from the shower, still buttoning his shirt in that carelessly immodest way of his. He looked at Deidre with a mixture of joy and surprise and said, "I didn't hear you come in."

Deidre, who was nineteen and had a French braid and gold hoop earrings, stirred the pot on the stove. "You were in the shower," she explained.

He sat down at the oak dinette table and gazed at her lovingly. "You could have come in there and announced yourself." He smirked.

She looked at him fondly. "I haven't got time to get into trouble with you today," she said. "I have a class this afternoon."

"Skip it," he said. "I'll give you a better education."

She laughed. "I'll bet you would. But you know I have to get good grades this year, so I can get into the CIA."

"You want to go off to New York and leave me." He pouted.

She turned from the stove, looking serious. "You could come with me."

They held each other's eyes. "You'd better be careful," he said. "I might take that invitation seriously."

"It would be good for your career," she told him. "That's what's holding you back, staying here in Florida."

"I'm not good enough for a club in Manhattan."

"You won't know that until you try. A change of scenery is probably just what you need."

"I need to be with you," he said. "If you go away, I'll self-destruct. I won't be able to eat or sleep or write anything. . . ."

"We don't have to think about this for another year," Deidre said quickly. "Let's just enjoy what we have now."

"You're right," he said. "What is that? It smells fantastic."

"Chili." She smiled because it was one of his favorites.

"You really spoil me, kid. Look at this. Flowers again."

"In Paris they buy flowers every week with the groceries."

"That's great. Hey. Let's run off to Paris."

"I told you"—she smiled, serving his lunch—"I have a class."

"Oh, that's right." He laughed. "Well, maybe tomorrow."

She sat across from him and took his hand. "I probably should run off with you," she said. "I've done wonders for you, you know, making you civilized and teaching you to eat lunch."

"That's right," he said. "Before you came along my life was a mess."

"Well, this apartment was, anyway! I can still remember the first time I saw it."

"You were just a little baby then," he teased, rubbing her knuckles with his thumb. "I didn't even think of you . . . as a woman. You were the answer to all my prayers and I was too dumb to see it. But then last Christmas, when you wore that red dress . . . I just . . . wow."

Deidre blushed. He was recalling the first time they'd made love. "I loved you from the first moment I saw you," she confessed. "I was so worried you wouldn't wait for me to grow up."

"Maybe that's what I was doing," he said thoughtfully. "All that time we were palling around, I never wanted to date other girls. Maybe I was secretly hoping and waiting for you."

"Maybe." She squeezed his hand and released it. "Eat your lunch now, Jeff, before it gets cold."

6

Palm trees shimmered in the atrium sunlight, casting fans of shadow across the table. There was a waterfall nearby; spiraling tiers of obsidian and mica rising from a pink-tiled pool. Soft breezes flowed from the air-conditioning ducts and ruffled the blossoms of the potted hibiscus. Faintly, along with the splashing and chair-scraping and the soft drone of conversation, stringed instruments played an unidentifiable song. Deidre loved the food court at the Coral Springs Mall above all places on earth. Everything was perfect there, controlled, man made, immortal. In spring the waterfall was banked with pots of daffodils and the walls bloomed with the colorful artwork of the local kindergartens. At Christmas there were galaxies of twinkly lights, clouds of angel's hair, and booming French horns. Now, in the heart of June, it was a tropical oasis.

Today, however, the quiet was a little disturbing because Susie was supposed to be talking about her date the night before. Instead she just sat there, hooking her hair behind her ear, sucking furiously on her straw, even though the drink was gone and the ice half-melted. Deidre considered herself good at drawing people out, but Susie was a special case. There was something almost forbidding about her when she wasn't ready to open up. Susie was the kind of person people described as sunny and cheerful and uncomplicated. But Deidre, who really knew her, understood that was mostly a trick for keeping everyone at a distance. At the core of Susie there was something nuclear that even Deidre was afraid to find out about. Maybe Susie herself didn't know what it was. But today it was visible in the vicious ice-sucking, in the impatient hair adjustments, in the eyes, cold and blue as marbles. So Deidre kept quiet and waited.

Susie suddenly jabbed at the ice in her cup. "Well, do you want to hear about it or not?" she said abruptly.

"Sure," Deidre said, keeping neutral.

Susie sighed deeply. "Okay. I told you I had to walk down the street and wait on the corner, right?"

"Yeah."

"Well, he was late. So after ten thousand mosquitoes bit me, Curt finally showed up and honked—he has a green Camaro—and just sort of leaned over and opened the passenger side. What do you think of that?"

Deidre blinked. "Camaros?"

Susie rattled her ice impatiently. "He didn't get out to open up my door!"

Deidre squirmed. Nothing unnerved her like displays of anger. Growing up, she had never seen any and she took them for cataclysmic events. "Well . . ." she said, almost defensively, "we don't believe in that anyway, do we?"

Susie made a noise. "He could go a little out of his way, since he made me wait for him on a *street corner*!"

"That was your idea!"

Susie's eyes flashed. "Whose side are you on?"

"I didn't know there were sides!"

Susie sat back. "I'm sorry. I'm sorry. I got in the car and he said he liked my outfit. I had on my black jeans and the yellow tank top . . . you know?"

"Yes, I know. Do you think you should have worn that top on the first date?"

"Well, it got his attention. He could hardly drive, he kept looking over at me. And then I said, 'Where are we going?' and he said, 'Let's just drive around.' And after a minute he asked me to lean over the gearshift so he could put his arm around me."

"Did you?"

"For a while. But I didn't like what his hand was doing so I told him it was too uncomfortable."

"What was his hand doing?"

"Well, he didn't put it on my arm or my shoulder. He sort of hung it around my neck right *here*." She indicated a level just above her breast. "He didn't touch it, but it just made me nervous, that hand *hanging* there."

Deidre fought back the urge to make a speech. "Uh-huh," she said.

"So anyway, we drove all around and talked a little, mostly about me—he didn't want to talk about himself —so I was telling him I wanted to be an actress and all that and I noticed he was running out of gas, probably on purpose so I told him he'd better fill up. And he said he didn't want to fill up because he didn't have much money and his dad took away his credit cards, so I said *I* would pay for it."

"Uh-huh," Deidre said.

"So after the gas station he said, 'Do you want to go to Mullins Park?' "

"Uh-huh."

"And I said yes."

There was a brief silence, punctuated by waterfall-splashing.

"And so . . ." Deidre said.

"So we went there. It was dark by that time and he put the car in park and started kissing me."

"Just like that? Without saying anything?"

"What would he say?"

"Well, I don't know, but what if you didn't want to do that?"

"I could have shoved him off or something. I don't know. I didn't want him to think I was a little kid."

"It doesn't sound like he thought that!"

"Well, anyway . . . Deidre . . . there's a lot more to kissing than you think."

Deidre had no idea how to respond to that.

"I mean . . . this guy . . . he can really . . . kiss. He was doing all this stuff . . . I can't even . . . it was really confusing."

"That's no time to be confused!" Deidre said. "What did he do?"

"Well, you know . . . with his tongue in my mouth."

"Did you like that?" Deidre asked, thirsting for information.

"*Yeah!* But what I didn't like was his hands were all over . . . I mean, he was going too fast, you know? Trying to get under my clothes and stuff. . . . I really wanted to enjoy myself, but that made me nervous, so I shoved him back. Kind of hard. And he said, 'What's wrong?' and I said, 'You're going too fast,' and he said he was sorry but he really liked me and he didn't know how much experience I had and he said, 'You can always tell me to stop and I'll stop.'"

"That's very generous of him," Deidre said dryly.

"Well, at least he said it! Anyway, I decided I needed to catch my breath so I said I was hungry. I mean, I just wanted to talk to him and get to know him a little better before . . . and he acted sort of hurt and said, 'Did I do something wrong? Did I do something you don't like?' and I said, 'No, no, I'm just hungry.' So we went to Burger King and he was really quiet. I mean, he would answer questions but that was it. And I said, 'Are you mad?' and he said, 'No, no, no.' But he was."

"See? You're just too young for him. You and he want different things."

"No, we don't. I want the same thing, I just want it *slower.*"

"Well, what happened after Burger King?"

"He said, 'Do you want to go home?' not real snotty but kind of, and I said yes because it was after ten and I didn't want my parents to get suspicious, so he drove me home in total silence and he stopped about a block from my house and said in that same voice, 'Can I kiss you good-night?' and I said, of course and he leaned over and gave me a kiss like you'd give your aunt or something, so I sort of kissed him the *other* way and this time he pulled back and he looked at me real confused and said, 'I guess you're trying to drive me crazy.' and I said, 'No, I'm not.' and he asked if I would go out with him again and I said yes and he asked if he could meet me here on his break today and I said yes and that's the whole story."

The waterfall splashed away. The Muzak was playing "Like a Virgin" in polka time.

"Well?" Susie asked.

"Well?" Deidre answered. "Do you want my honest opinion? I think he's kind of a sleazy person. I don't think you should go out with him anymore. He just wants one thing."

"Oh, I knew you'd say something like that!"

"Well, you didn't have a good time! You should be happy right now, but you look like a coiled-up snake!

You're sitting here grinding that poor helpless ice . . . you tell me what to think!"

"I know he's . . . too interested in sex, but there's more to him than that."

"Like what?" Deidre sneered. "You think behind all that is a deep, sensitive guy?"

"Maybe! I'd like to find out."

"Susie, you're wrong. I thought you were wrong in the first place and I'm sure now. This guy just wants to jump you. He picked you out because you're young and you don't know how to fight him off. The girls his own age have probably all told him to get lost."

Susie stirred the ice in her cup. "I hear you," she said. "You might be right. But I'm not ready to give up yet. I mean, I know, yes, he has that problem, but why do I still like him?"

"Because you're crazy."

"Well, that's one reason I decided to meet him here today. I want you to look at him again."

"Okay." Deidre sighed.

"Now, what's all this about you being in love?"

"Let me tell you about my *mom* first. The other thing I don't even know if I should talk about."

"Oh, yes, you will."

"Anyway! Mom is dating this guy she works for. He's an accountant. And last night she had him over for dinner, so I got to meet him."

Susie's eyes were wide with interest. "Is it serious?"

"I have no idea. He kissed her."

"Boy! It must be weird having a *parent* who's doing that stuff. My mom better not . . . anyway, what's he like?"

"Short, thin, well dressed . . ."

"A nerd?"

"No! I liked him. He's really intelligent and he was very nice to me. You know, he didn't act like I was just some kid he had to put up with. But here's the strange thing. Mom kept picking fights with him."

"About what?"

"You name it. It was like . . . I don't know. It was weird."

"Some people show affection that way."

"Come on. My mom? I've never seen her like this. She really pounced all over this guy."

"Well, don't expect me to explain older people. I think they all go nuts around forty. The other day Sondra and I were sitting in the living room, minding our own business, watching Home Shopping, and Mom comes in and says, 'I want to tell you about our family history.' She starts in on how we came from Bavaria and I don't know what all. It was *macabre*."

"It must be scary to get old."

"They think too much at that age. That's their trouble. Look how my dad went bananas. Come on now, I've been patient. What about your guy?"

Deidre put her hands on the table and laced her fingers together. "He's not my guy. It isn't anything like that. I met this . . . person and I really like him, but I don't know if anything is going to happen. . . ." Deidre hesitated. There was something frightening about telling it. It was like a magic spell that might be broken. "Well . . ." she began again in a low voice.

There was a violent commotion next to her and Deidre screamed involuntarily. Curt Wyler had appeared out of nowhere and hurled himself into a chair so hard, it skidded and nearly tipped over. After this violent entrance he ignored the two girls, slumping and glaring at the waterfall from beneath his satanic eyebrows. "Fuck," he muttered to himself.

While Deidre got over the shock of this, Susie folded her arms, gearing up for battle. "Anything wrong?" she asked sarcastically.

He made a noise like a horse snorting.

Deidre was admiring the beautiful lines of his slumping shoulders. Then she realized he was wearing a long-sleeved river-driver's shirt. That seemed like an odd choice for a ninety-degree day.

After a while Curt swiveled and looked at his companions. "Hi," he said to Deidre. "I'm sorry," he said to Susie. "I'm in a bad mood. I just got fired."

"Fired!" Susie squeaked. "You're kidding. Why?"

"Why!" he said with contempt. "Because the world is *fucked* is why. Because God hates me. Because my whole life—"

"What happened?" Susie interrupted.

"I came in late." He glowered at the table.

"She fired you for that?"

"It wasn't the first time." He put his head on his hands. "It's not her fault. It's my *father's* fault."

"Why?" Deidre asked softly. She found herself liking him better, strangely, now that he was so upset. Maybe because he was being himself instead of putting on an act.

"He wouldn't let me out of the goddamn *house* is why!" he shouted. "He had so much to tell me about what a fuck-up I am. There aren't enough hours in the day for that."

"Why didn't you just leave?" Susie asked.

He looked at her as if she were crazy. "Come to my house and try that," he said. "And now! *Now* when I tell him I lost another job, I'm going to get it all over again. God, I hate that man!" He covered his face with both hands.

Susie touched his arm lightly. "You don't mean that," she said.

"Don't!" He shook her off violently. "How do you know what I mean?"

No one spoke. The Muzak was now playing a mocking rendition of "Don't Worry, Be Happy."

Deidre felt sorry for him, but Susie seemed annoyed by the whole thing. She turned to Deidre as if she were finished with Curt. "Go on with what you were saying," she prompted.

"Not now!" Deidre said without thinking.

Curt looked up from his hands, dazed. "Oh, great.

You guys don't want me either? Fine." He pushed his chair back.

"No, wait," Deidre said. "Don't go."

"Let him, if he wants to," Susie said.

Curt looked at her poisonously. "You're sweet," he said.

"Well, what do you expect? You come over here out of nowhere and throw a tantrum and don't even say hello."

"Hello!" he said bitterly.

"Hello," she said coldly.

Curt turned to Deidre. "I'm really sorry. I was just so pissed off. If you guys are talking about something private, I can leave. I'm not going to go cut my wrists or anything."

Deidre was torn between compassion and shyness. "No, it's okay," she said. "I was just going to tell Susie about this guy I met."

For the first time that day Curt stopped scowling. "Yeah? That sounds interesting."

"Well . . ." Deidre said uncertainly. She decided to look only at Susie. "A couple of weeks ago I met this man by the pool at our building."

"Man?" Susie inquired.

"Well, yes, that's the thing," Deidre said, looking down. "I think he's in his twenties somewhere."

"Somewhere?" Susie voice got higher and higher.

"Well, I haven't asked him his exact age!" Deidre said. "He lives in the apartment above mine and he plays the piano in the bar of a Holiday Inn in Fort Lauderdale."

"I think I saw this movie on HBO!" Curt chuckled.

"Shut up," Susie told him. "Dee-Dee!" she said. "I can't believe this. You gave me a hard time about going out with somebody Curt's age!"

"She did?" Curt asked.

"Just a little!" Deidre said. She was ready to kill everyone at that point. "Anyway, it's not the same. I'm not dating this guy. We're just friends."

"Does he have a lot of fourteen-year-old girls for friends?" Curt asked. " 'Cause I'd like to meet him and get some pointers."

"I just like him!" Deidre said. "That's all there is to it. I've been up to his apartment and we've talked a couple of times and he's really neat. I admire him. He writes music and everything." She was sorry she'd told. The whole thing sounded like a silly fantasy. They couldn't possibly understand what it was really like with her and Jeff, how it was a special thing that didn't fit in any category.

"Where do you say he works?" Curt asked. "Some Holiday Inn?"

"Yes," Deidre said defiantly. "He's really too good for that but—"

"Let's go see him," Curt said. "Does he work tonight?"

"No, he doesn't work on Sundays," Deidre said,

stunned by the concept that she could actually go and see Jeff work.

"They wouldn't let us in the bar anyway," Susie said.

"Sure they would," Curt replied. "Anybody can *sit* in a bar. We just order soft drinks and nobody will say anything."

Deidre's heart began to pound. She didn't know if she wanted this or not. It was the kind of decision she would have liked to ponder for weeks. "Really?" she asked meekly.

"Sure. It's a *hotel*, for Christ's sake. We can say something like we're there with our parents on vacation and they went out and we want to see the show. Then if we don't act rowdy or cause them any trouble, they'll let us sit there. A hotel bar is the easiest kind to crash. Come on, I need a night out with two beautiful women. That's *just* what I need. Tomorrow night. Okay?"

Susie's mood was perking up with a possible adventure on the horizon. "It's up to Deidre," she said.

Curt looked at Deidre. She felt trapped and thrilled and terrified at the same time. "What do you wear in a place like that?" she asked.

"Wear!" Curt scoffed. "Wear whatever you goddamn want. It's darker than the inside of a goat in those dumps. Half the customers are doing it under the table."

That settled it for Susie. "Come on, Dee, let's live dangerously. This'll be great."

"Okay," Deidre said. She couldn't resist this extraordinary opportunity to see Jeff in a new setting. But still she was scared. As if showing Jeff to her friends might make him disappear.

"Well, Curtis," Susie said, "since you did a favor for my cousin and had a great idea, I've decided to forgive you for all your sins." She leaned on his arm.

"Don't!" he cried, just like before, pulling back. Then he actually blushed. "I'm sorry. I hurt that arm this morning. Grab me on the other side."

Susie scooted her chair to the other side. "How'd you hurt your arm?"

He looked down at the table. "I fell out of bed," he said.

Susie laughed. "Klutz!" She leaned on his good arm.

Curt looked up anxiously. "Have you guys had lunch? I'll buy you a pizza."

"Are you sure you want to do that if you just lost your job?" Deidre asked.

"Why not?" he said. "Might as well spend it while I still have it." He got up so quickly, they had to hurry to follow him. "Anyway," he mumbled, "I'm not in a tremendous hurry to get home."

7

Deidre didn't care if the Sundowner Lounge was darker than the inside of a goat or not. This was a royal occasion and she was going to dress royally. There was, she felt, a vague chance Jeff might actually see her in the audience or even come sit with them between sets, and she wanted to convey the correct impression—that she was a sharp young woman with sharp young friends who went to trendy bars and cafés all the time. She had the dress—a black cotton knit tank. She knew if she'd had the guts she would put black Reeboks with it, but she didn't have the guts, so she went with a pair of clogs that were clunky enough to get by. The purse was easy. Once, on impulse, and because Susie had pressured her, she'd spent two months' allowance on a neon-pink disco bag with fringe, which now sat guiltily in the back of her closet. The final, most critical element was jewelry. It was like seasoning in cooking. There were so many ways to go—trashy, flashy, antique . . . Should she wear a stack of pink bracelets to match the purse or was that too obvious? Big earrings were trite, as were pearls or clusters of pins. There had to be something new to do. By Monday afternoon she was frantic over this point, trying on and discarding everything in her jewelry box. She should have asked Susie to go shopping, but she didn't want to act like she was trying too hard. To add to her anxiety Jeff began to practice upstairs around four o'clock. He played "It Must Have Been Love" over and over, trying different tempos and styles. Maybe he was working it up for tonight.

"What kind of jewelry do you like?" Deidre asked the ceiling. She tried to remember the picture of his former girlfriend, but she had been wearing a swimsuit, so she wasn't well accessorized.

Out of sheer desperation Deidre went to her mother's room. Mrs. Holland had every piece of jewelry she'd ever owned, all jumbled and dumped together in her bottom dresser drawer. All she ever wore—her watch and a set of pearls—she kept in a glass box on top of her dresser. Deidre had found treasures in her mother's Lost Jewelry Collection before: a real surfer's cross, and an Indian-looking necklace of aqua beads. Maybe there was some perfect piece in there waiting to be discovered. Usually she got her mother's permission to look through her things, but she felt that was just a formality. Her mother wouldn't miss any of the stuff anyway, and besides, Deidre was feeling just a little annoyed with her mother at that moment. Yesterday, when she'd asked permission to go out tonight, she'd been all prepared to defend herself and answer questions. She'd worked out a careful story about "going out with a group of friends to see a concert." Then she braced herself for the questions that could unravel her story: What kind of concert? Which friends? What ages? But her mother had simply said, "Oh, that works out great. Because I have a bunch of things to catch up on at work. I'll just have dinner at the office. What time will you be home?" That was it. Deidre could have been headed for the Pure Platinum Club to participate in Amateur Jell-O Night. She could have gone to the Strip and turned tricks. She could have observed satanic rituals and made human sacrifices. As long as she promised to come home at a certain time. It was infuriating. It either meant her mother thought she was too goody good to come up with any plans worth investigating or that her mother was too excited about the prospect of spending more time with Mr. Maxwell to think straight. Either way, she didn't seem to be taking her role as a parent very seriously. "Eleven?" Deidre had said, hoping her mother would at least bargain for ten. But Mrs. Holland only wavered a second. "Okay, but not a minute later." So, in a way Deidre felt she was owed something.

Still she felt guilty, even entering her mother's room without permission. The piano music was louder here, since she was closer to the living room. Jeff was back on Billy Joel again, playing "Just the Way You Are."

Her mother's room was not messy, exactly, just poorly organized. She never threw anything away and there was a weird accumulation of things from different phases of her life. The walls were covered with photos of Deidre at various ages, a watercolor Mrs. Holland had done in high school, of horses running, her enlarged wedding picture, an Irish blessing some co-worker had given her years ago, a crayon drawing Deidre made in the second grade, and a print of da Vinci's "Last Supper." Every available space, including windowsills, was crowded with Deidre's childhood craftwork, along with little pieces of art glass collected from fairs and carnivals. On the gold bedspread was a huge stuffed white cat, an early courtship present from Deidre's father. On the dresser, along with the photo of Mr. Holland in uniform, was a huge vase of artificial daisies and gladiolas. The room smelled like Mrs. Holland's cologne, tangerines and cloves. Deidre breathed in the atmosphere and all the childhood memories it evoked, then knelt on the floor in front of the dresser and opened the bottom drawer. Jeff was now playing "When Something Is Wrong with My Baby."

The drawer always reminded Deidre of that scene in *Treasure Island* where they go into the cave and see the piles and piles of treasure. Late-afternoon sun slanted in, illuminating the drawer and making it seem almost magical. Deidre lifted a strand of amber beads and held them to the light. Interesting, she thought, but no good on a black dress at night. She hesitated over some simulated jade earrings, then noticed a little plaid button. She remembered the plaid, from one of her old dresses. Probably around first grade. She had been impressed with the fabric-covered buttons. Her mother must have cut this off and kept it for a souvenir after Deidre outgrew the dress. Maybe she should forgive her mother after all—she was absentminded, not neglectful. She obviously loved Deidre—the whole room was a testament to that.

Then Deidre saw something in the drawer she'd never seen before. It was an envelope with the flap tucked in, rather than sealed. There was no writing on it, but still, Deidre knew it was something private. She knew full well she would be furious if her mother went in her room and looked through things. But Deidre couldn't control herself. It was that "curious nature." She opened the flap and a dozen or so scraps of paper fell out. They were little notes, all folded in half, all written in a tiny, precise script that looked like typewriting. All from the same notepad, headed *From the Desk of Henry Maxwell.* Deidre opened and read each one quickly, before her conscience could stop her.

> **Help! This asshole is boring me to death. Come in in five minutes and interrupt with something. Yours, HM**

> **What did you do to your hair this morning? It looks hot. Respectfully, HM**

Dear Associate. My mouth gets me in a lot of trouble. Am I in trouble with you? Yours? HM

My Dear Mrs. Holland. How do you feel about inter-office dating? Your answer will not affect your current review. HM

Dear Mrs. Holland—in answer to your recent inquiry, I sure as hell do. Fondly, HM

Dear Janet. Thanks.

Jan—Come in my office, if you get a minute. I need a little more "inspiration." Your humble servant, HM

Dear Jan—I won't be in till after lunch so feel free to goof off, talk on phone, etc. I decided I need a haircut. I'm scared to death about meeting your kid. Analyze that. HM

Jan—Let's have dinner soon. Okay?

Deidre read them over and over, trying to imagine the various situations in which they'd been written. What was he thanking her for? Apologizing for? Were these the words of a man in love or just casually dating? She couldn't figure any of it out except that he was nervous about meeting *her*. Did that mean he was so serious, he was thinking about being her stepfather? Deidre's stomach twisted. It was so weird. She liked Mr. Maxwell. She wanted her mother to be happy, but . . . She looked up at the top of the dresser, at the picture of her father. He wasn't like a real person to her, because he'd died when she was two. Shot in the line of duty. In another drawer Deidre's mom kept all that stuff—his citation, his shield, his love letters. Deidre remembered what her mother had said about Mr. Maxwell: *He's nothing like your father.* Did that mean he fell short in some way? It was frustrating. Here was something that might affect Deidre's whole life and she couldn't figure it out. Mr. Maxwell's notes weren't exactly love letters, but her mother was *saving* them. What was going on?

It was quiet upstairs now. Jeff was probably taking a break. He practiced intensely in the late afternoons. She supposed he slept late in the mornings. That was what she had always heard about musicians. If they got married, it would be fine, because as a restaurant owner Deidre would have the same kind of hours.

She carefully put Mr. Maxwell's notes where she'd found them. Then she saw the perfect piece of jewelry —a large enamel pin in the shape of a flamingo. Her mother had probably picked it up at some Florida crafts fair. She took it and left quickly, anxious to get back to her own room where the atmosphere was less confusing.

I

Curt and Susie picked Deidre up at seven. She was glad to see they had dressed well—Curt was in black and silver, going for a south Florida version of Santa Fe. Susie, as usual, was mocking the sixties with patterned leggings and earrings like industrial light fixtures. Since Jeff didn't sing until nine o'clock, Curt said they should eat something at the Holiday Inn coffee shop. He felt it was important they be seen around the hotel, so they could safely pose as guests. During dinner he briefed the girls on bar-crashing strategy.

"There are two key points to remember," he told them. "Number one, don't lie about anything you don't have to, and two, don't cause any kind of trouble. If we get loud or silly, or *giggle*, that's it. But if we stay inconspicuous, no problem. Okay, the story is, we're here on vacation with our parents. They went out and we're bored and we want to see the show. We're all brothers and sisters. We're underage, which we freely admit, and we drink sodas. Susie, you've got to make a real effort to act mature. I figure you're our weak link."

"What does that mean?" she cried indignantly.

"Well, Muffin, I hate to tell you, but you've got a voice like the whole brass section of an orchestra and you laugh too loud and you get too excited. We've got to stay quiet."

"I can be as quiet as I want to!" Susie shouted.

He sighed. "And another thing, *sis*. No fooling around under the table. I don't care how dark it is. You have to act like my sweet baby sister."

"You're the one with the problem in that department!" Susie said.

"Why doesn't anyone think *I* could cause any problems?" Deidre asked, rather hurt.

"Christ," Curt said. "Why do I let myself in for this stuff?"

"Because you want to see Dee-Dee's boyfriend as much as I do," Susie said.

"He's not—" Deidre began.

"All right." Curt looked at his watch. "It's almost eight-thirty. I think we'd better go in now and get established. There's an outside chance they'll be really paranoid and kick us out right away and we don't want that to happen during Mr. Wonderful's act. But if we sit there awhile and act harmless, we're home free."

Susie grabbed Deidre's arm. "This is so exciting!" she cried shrilly.

"We're doomed," Curt muttered. He got up. "Follow me, Girl Scouts. Let me do all the talking and act like you've got nothing to hide."

Deidre stood up. Other than leg tremors and a mild heart attack, she was doing fine.

The Sundowner Lounge was across the hall from the coffee shop. As Curt had predicted, it was very dark inside. Canned music and cigarette smoke billowed from its cavelike doorway. Just outside there was a men's room and a long row of pay telephones, all getting heavy use.

Curt sauntered into the smoky darkness as if it were second nature. He made a gesture to the girls, indicating a table he liked, near the back, sheltered from the stage by a pillar. "Quick getaway," he whispered. He sat down. "Sit up straight and look respectful," he continued. "Don't look like anybody's idea of a bad kid." He glanced around. "What a break! Waitresses." He pulled the candle from the middle of the table close to his side, so he was illuminated. "When they see how cute I am, we'll be in business."

"I think I'm going to be sick," Susie said.

Deidre was studying the room. As her eyes adjusted to the darkness, she saw clusters of little tables, like theirs, and a strange number of those pillars, whose only purpose seemed to be to block the view from one table to another. Front and center was the stage—a raised platform with a piano and microphone already set up. In front of that was a tiny, inlaid dance floor. All along the far wall was the bar, shiny as a fire engine with its brass and chrome and leather. The bartender and all the waitresses were female, blond, and dressed in black. They could have been sisters. Deidre instantly wondered if Jeff was friendly with any of them. The customers, so far, were all men. There was a large group of men in suits, who had pulled their ten chairs up to a tiny table for four and who were obviously trying to outdo each other at getting drunk and cutting loose. There were two very handsome young men, drinking beer together and having an intense conversation that looked like an argument. There was a man about thirty, all alone, so drunk he could hardly sit up on his chair, who gazed at his shoes and laughed occasionally. Finally, there were several men of varying ages and types up at the bar, all vying for the attention of the bartender. All in all it gave the song "Piano Man" new meaning. The mood in here clearly was closer to desperation than to fun.

One of the blond waitress-droids approached their table and frowned. She had a tattoo of a butterfly on her arm. "What's this?" she demanded.

Unruffled, Curt sat up straighter. "What's what?" he asked.

She shifted the tray she was holding. "Toys 'R' Us is down the street," she said flatly.

"Okay, I know," Curt said, shifting his personality a little to match hers. "But could you give us a little break? I have to baby-sit these guys."

"You are *not* baby-sitting!" cried Susie, who had taken acting classes. "Big jerk!"

"Mom left me in charge!" Curt argued convincingly.

Susie stuck out her tongue.

"We've already had some wonderful cuisine from the coffee shop and my parents said we can't leave the hotel," Curt went on, smiling at the waitress. "We've seen all the HBO movies and they've used up all their quarters on the Magic Fingers and I could really use a ginger ale."

"And we heard you had a really good show down here," Deidre put in.

The waitress chomped her gum like a cow. Despite a lot of makeup she didn't really look much older than Curt. "The show's for adults, sweetie," she said. "Just like this bar is."

"*Please* give me a break," Curt said. "I can't tie them up in the lobby, can I? I promise they'll be good."

"I don't want to get in trouble," she said, fooling with her earring. "Go buy them some ice cream."

"Oh, come on, show me some mercy," Curt said. "I'm a big tipper." He smiled suggestively.

She shifted her weight, looking at him anew. "Oh, yeah? Well, okay, big man, but if anybody acts up, you're outta here. Got it?"

"Yes, ma'am," Curt said sweetly. "Ginger ale, please."

"Seven-Up and grenadine," said Susie.

"Jeez," said the waitress.

"Coke," Deidre said.

She wrote this down and looked at Curt again. "You staying here long?" she asked.

He smiled meltingly. "Could be. Maybe I'll see you around sometime."

"You never know." She smiled back, slapping the bill down. She deliberately put some extra swing in her walk as she left them.

Susie punched Curt on the arm. "You're in *big* trouble!"

"Ouch! *Dammit!* I hate it when you do that! We got to stay, didn't we? I'm doing all this for Deidre!" He looked at his watch. "Five minutes to nine, kid," he said.

"Oh, God," Deidre said softly.

Susie grabbed at her hand. "This is so exciting!" she squeaked. "I can't wait to see him!"

"Shh," Curt said. "Come on, now. You promised."

The waitress returned. "Vernor's," she recited, setting things down. "Kiddie cocktail and The Real Thing. Nicki thought you'd enjoy the garbage." She pointed to the bartender, who waved to them. She'd put a cherry in the ginger ale, lime wedge in Deidre's Coke, and a pink umbrella in Susie's drink. Deidre was touched.

"You just whistle if you want anything else." She smiled at Curt, sauntering off.

Deidre picked up her lime wedge, which was impaled on a toothpick. "Do you eat this?" she asked.

"Christ, no!" Curt said. "Put it back and act like a grown-up!"

"This really works!" Susie exclaimed, opening and closing her umbrella.

"Doomed," Curt muttered.

Any minute now. Deidre's coronary system was out of control. She realized he was already on the premises somewhere. She looked at the room one more time. One of the businessmen was drawing or writing something on a napkin, while the others peered over his shoulder, giggling. The drunk was even drunker now, sitting on his spine. "What?" he said, although no one had spoken to him. One of the handsome young men had lost his temper and was getting up to go, but the other one caught his wrist and made him hesitate. The crowd at the bar was larger and a woman had finally

come in, a good-looking middle-aged lady in a gold
lamé top. Half the men who had been trying to pick up
the bartender were now working on her, but she ignored them, brushing them off like flies.

A bright spotlight hit the stage. The angry young
man sat down again. The businessmen put away their
drawings.

The bartender sprinted up and took the microphone
from its stand. "Good evening and welcome to the Sundowner Lounge. I'm Nicki Adams and I'm pleased to
welcome all of you here tonight." She paused, as if
waiting for a response. "We've got some good stuff for
you tonight, a little boy named Jeff Elliot, who I person-
ally have a big crush on." She paused to let the crowd
laugh. "And he also has some talent, so what more do
you want? Welcome with me, please . . . Jeff Elliot!"

There was sketchy applause. Jeff appeared out of the
darkness in a white sport coat and a yellow T-shirt.
"Hi!" he said to the group, giving them the puppyish
look Deidre knew well. "Can you see me okay? Is there
only one of me?" He waited while they laughed. He
raised his hand. "How many people wish this was the
Westin? I do. Because *I'd* be getting more money." He
sat down at the piano, let the laughter fade, and then
looked at them coyly. "And *you'd* be getting a better
show."

He had a nice rapport with them. They liked him.
Deidre felt a strange pang of jealousy, realizing his

charm was something he tossed away casually to the public at large. It was nothing special he saved for her.

Then he looked over his shoulder at the bar. "You're not going to tell the management of Holiday Inn I said that, are you?"

Nicki shook her head no, laughing.

"Good," he said. "Okay, here's what I do. I'm going to play some stuff I like, but if you have a request, bring it up, if you want to dance, dance. If you want to be sick, leave! And when I take my breaks, if anybody wants to buy me a drink, that's okay."

"I'll buy you one!" Gold-Lamé called out.

Jeff did an elaborate double-take. "Hmmm," he said. "Maybe I'm glad I'm not at the Westin after all. But enough about me. . . ." He began to play and sing "Little Child."

Deidre realized she'd never heard him sing before. He had a nice voice, tenor and sweetly vulnerable. As always, his piano playing was superb. The crowd slowly resumed their conversations, treating him as background music. The waitresses began to move around again, freshening up orders.

"My God!" Susie said, turning breathlessly to Deidre. "Do you really know him? Are you really friends with him?"

"How old is he?" Curt asked, in an awed tone of voice.

"I don't know," Deidre said softly. She couldn't take her eyes off the stage. It was like some kind of dream.

She didn't believe it, either, that she was really friends with this . . . adult. It was so strange to see him in his blinding white jacket, with that bright light glaring on him. He looked so . . . what was the word? She watched his knuckles moving gracefully up and down the keyboard. His facial expression was soft, thoughtful, lost in the meaning of the song. What kind of courage did it take to get up there night after night and *sing* in front of these benignly disinterested people?

"He's really good looking," she heard Susie say.

"He's good too. He sounds good," Curt said.

"Do you really know him?" Susie asked again.

Deidre listened to the words and music, spiraling into the air like cigarette smoke. "I don't *know,*" she said quietly. "I don't know."

I

At ten forty-five Jeff began his fourth and final set. The crowd had thinned considerably. The businessmen had gone on to another bar. The two handsome men had left at ten, with their arms around each other. A young couple had come in and were drinking champagne and holding hands and requesting love songs to dance to. The drunk was still there and so was the gold-lamé lady, who had bought drinks for Jeff during each one of his breaks. Deidre, who was too scared to make her presence known during those intervals, had grown to hate the woman. Overaged groupie.

In fact, all night long Deidre had been afraid he

would come toward the back of the room and see her, but he never did. When he wasn't onstage he went right to the bar and sat with his back to the room. She was relieved, but also a little disappointed.

"You guys, we've got to leave right now," Curt said. "I said I'd have you both back by eleven and we're going to be late as it is."

"I don't care," Deidre said. "I want to see the last set. My mom doesn't care what I do anyway."

"I want to stay too," said Susie, who had convinced herself she was drunk on grenadine.

The young couple requested "Blame It on Midnight" and began to dance, hanging and clinging on each other. The drunk pulled a chair up under his legs, making a bed for himself. The gold-lamé lady got up and danced by herself, trying to put on a show for Jeff, Deidre felt.

Nicki was tidying things up. She went over to the drunk and knelt beside him, speaking in whispers. He took a huge handful of money out of his pocket and gave it to her, rolled off the chairs, rested on his knees a moment, then stood up and drifted out into the night.

The waitress came over to Curt. "Okay," she said. "I've been a sport, but it's curfew time now. You kids better go on up to your room. If you're down here after eleven, we might really get in trouble."

"We just want to stay till the end of the show," Deidre said. She wanted to see if Jeff would leave with that woman. She was slithering all around the dance floor like a gold reptile, trying to get his attention. Deidre was sure she was some kind of old ex-hooker or stripper or something. Surely Jeff wouldn't go for something like that!

"Okay, okay," said the waitress, clearing up their glasses. "You've been pretty good." They had too. They had had two drinks apiece and even Susie had been relatively quiet, stunned into silence by the magnitude of Deidre's choice of men. Curt handed the waitress a credit card.

"Did you get your dad's permission to use his card?" Susie asked, when the waitress was gone.

He laughed. "Right," he said. "He's rich. He'll never miss it."

Jeff finished his song. He looked just a little tired. "Okay, kids," he said, to the three people on the dance floor. "This is the grand finale. What do you want?"

"I want *you*!" Gold-Lamé sang out. She had a southern accent, too, the bitch.

Jeff just laughed. "I don't know that one. Anyway, I was talking to the newlyweds."

The man smiled, looking into the woman's eyes. " 'It Had to Be You.' "

"Nice choice," Jeff approved. And he sang it so softly and sweetly, Deidre ached to jump up and run to him.

The waitress brought back the check and Curt signed his father's name and left a large tip.

When the song was over, Deidre had tears in her

eyes. Partly because of his singing, but mostly because she didn't want the evening to come to an end.

"Let's go," Curt said briskly. "Really. I'm going to get killed as it is."

"One more minute," Deidre said. The honeymoon couple drifted out together. Jeff took off his jacket and slung it over his shoulder, exposing his arms and upper body to Gold-Lamé, who was just standing there on the dance floor. He ignored her, turning his back and gathering up his things.

Curt saw what was going on. "Come on, Deidre," he said. "He's a big boy. He can take care of himself."

The woman climbed the steps to the stage and sat on Jeff's piano bench. She leaned back against the keys, rhythmically slipping one shoe on and off. She said something that made Jeff laugh.

"I have to see what happens," Deidre said, wishing he hadn't turned the microphone off. He looked so beautiful in that yellow T-shirt, damn him.

"Come on, Dee," Susie said, taking her arm. "If that's what he wants to do, you can't stop him anyway."

"I . . ." Deidre choked up.

"Come on." Curt went swiftly to her side and helped her stand up. Susie came around to the other side. Deidre didn't know if they were trying to comfort her or prevent her from making a scene.

"I'm not jealous," she said, trying to resist their gentle pulling. "I'm just concerned." She looked hopefully at the stage, now really wishing he'd see her, but his back was still turned. He said something that made the woman laugh.

"Come on, Dee," Susie said.

"Stop treating me like a mental patient!" Deidre said, shaking them both off. Still he didn't look around. Was he deaf?

Curt put his arm firmly around her shoulders and led her into the blinding light of the lobby. It was so bright, her eyes filled up with tears.

She got home late but it didn't make any difference because her mother was still out. Deidre went straight to bed, but she couldn't fall asleep. She kept trying to hear some sounds from upstairs, to indicate when he came in, but it was all silent.

8

Everyone said it was the hottest new club in Manhattan. The owner, a Miamian, had taken the best elements of South Florida style and polished them up for the big city. There was a spare, dark elegance in the old-fashioned cocktails they served and the little Latin coffees. The walls, tables, chairs, and Jeff's piano were all black lacquer. Against this stark backdrop tropical colors bloomed in the neon that gave the club its name. A band of aqua coursed around the ceiling and floor, like molding. Lime framed the exits. Amber ran up and down the bar. The stage and piano were edged in brilliant soda-pink. On each table a single orchid floated in a neon-edged bowl. The best table in the house, closest to the stage, was reserved permanently for Deidre, who came almost every night, if she didn't have an exam in the morning. Sometimes she brought her friends from the Culinary Institute, but often she came alone. Jeff always complained bitterly about the nights she wasn't there. She brought him luck, he said.

She was there tonight, in a new black dress with sequins. She wore a lot of black, was getting known for it. Her hair was the usual French braid and she wore a diamond stud in one ear. Jeff had given her the set last Christmas, but she refused to wear them both at once. She tried to persuade Jeff to wear the other, but he said he was too old for that. He said he'd leave it to her to make the fashion statements.

"Everything okay, Deidre?" asked her waiter. All the waiters knew her name.

"Yes, thank you, Tom." She showed him her scarcely touched martini. She disliked alcohol, so she usually nursed one drink all evening long. She chose martinis for the shape of the glass and because she liked olives.

"Let me know if you need anything," he said, giving her a warm smile. He had asked her out once, before anyone had explained to him about her and Jeff. Maybe he was still hopeful. He was probably about her age, she guessed. Next to Jeff he seemed like a kid.

"I'll call you if I need you," she said dismissively. She opened her black beaded bag and took out a gold compact. She liked to check her face before the show started. Jeff looked at her for inspiration.

The piped-in jazz softened and faded out. Deidre sat up. A pink spotlight hit the stage. The club's owner, Frank Ippolito, mounted the stage and took the microphone. He was a very handsome older man with a low-

key kind of a charm and a soft, sexy voice. He reminded Deidre of a cat purring. "Good evening, ladies and gentlemen. Welcome to Neon. I hope you're enjoying the night. We have some extra pleasure for you now, one of the best young pianists in town whom we were lucky enough to discover about a year ago. We're doing all we can to keep him, so help me out, make him feel loved. Jeff Elliot."

Jeff appeared, looking, as always, faintly embarrassed by his applause. He grinned at Mr. Ippolito as they passed each other. Then he sat down at the piano, smiled and winked at Deidre, and turned his attention to his audience. His white suit was tinted a luscious strawberry color by the lights, as were his fair skin and hair. "Thank you," he said to quiet the applause. "Before I begin tonight I'd like to acknowledge the beautiful young lady at Table One, who also happens to be the love of my life and the inspiration for everything I do."

The spotlight moved to include Deidre, who was thrown. He'd never done anything like that before. The audience applauded her and she ducked her head. The spotlight made flashes of pink lightning in her dress.

"She's beautiful, isn't she?" Jeff asked the audience as the applause died down. "Her name is Deidre and this is for her."

The song was "Dancing in the Dark," one of her favorites. The spotlight stayed on both of them as he played and he played it so beautifully, Deidre couldn't

*help crying. She looked at him with tears in her eyes
and he gave her his warmest smile. She knew she had
made a big difference in his life. This was his way of
saying thank you.*

*When he finished, the audience applauded wildly,
showing their approval for love and romance. Deidre
broke down, touching the corners of her eyes with a
napkin.*

*"Isn't she something?" Jeff asked the audience, over
the applause. "That's my baby."*

I

Someone knocked. Deidre sat up in bed, her heart
beating fast, as if she'd been caught doing something
shameful.

"Hi," said her mother, coming in. "Did I wake you
up?"

"Yes," Deidre said, so her look of disorientation
would make sense.

"I'm sorry. I just wanted to *see* you. I got in so late last
night. How was the concert?"

"Fine. We had fun."

"Good. You were asleep when I got in and I didn't
want to wake you. We had an awful night. One of those
big snarly problems you can't untangle without going
over a million little details."

"Oh. Did you eat dinner?"

"Yes. Henry said he thought he deserved a steak. He

did, too, poor thing. He works too hard. When he isn't working, he's worrying about work."

"At least he eats steak while he worries," Deidre observed.

"Yeah. That part was nice. He wants to know if the two of us can go on a picnic with him Saturday. He seems to want to get to know you better."

"That sounds like he's serious about you."

"Oh, no, I doubt that. Do you want to?"

"Sure. Let me make the picnic. Then I'll really have fun."

"No argument here. Well, I've got to go."

"Say hi to Mr. Maxwell for me."

"Okay." As Mrs. Holland left the room, Deidre noticed even her *walk* was different these days, swishier. Then she realized it was because she was wearing heels. That seemed like a funny thing to do when dating such a short man. There were a lot of things about the adult world Deidre felt she didn't understand.

While she showered and dressed, she planned the picnic. Cold herbed chicken? Or cold barbecued chicken? Barbecued. Potato salad with oil and vinegar so it wouldn't spoil. Bread . . . what kind of bread? Something fruity or vegetably. And a great dessert. Mr. Maxwell liked chocolate, but he liked berries too. Raspberries and kir! Red peppers in the potato salad. That took care of fruits and vegetables. Dessert . . . Bread . . . Pound cake with chocolate syrup! *Bread.* Biscuits? Too crumbly. Come on, think . . .

The telephone rang. Deidre wrapped up in a towel and ran to answer it.

"Hi. Were you up?" It was Susie.

"Yeah."

"I just woke up. I've got a terrible hangover from last night."

"Get out of here!"

"Really. Everything goes to my head. Even grenadine."

"Susie. I don't even think there's alcohol in grenadine."

"Yes, there is. A little. I think. What else could be giving me this splitting headache?"

"Your overactive imagination?"

"Never mind that. What I wanted to say is . . . wow!"

Deidre smiled. "You mean Jeff?"

"He's . . . incredible. Are you really friends with him?"

"I've been up in his apartment."

"Wow. Do you think something will really happen?"

"I don't know. He likes me. He told me I was sweet."

"Wow. How can I get Curt to say something like that?"

"I don't know. Curt's a whole different kind of guy."

"I'll say. After we dropped you off he turned into an octopus again."

"His glands must be stuck. What did you do?"

"Like before. I pushed him off."

"What'd he do?"

"Like before. Clammed up. Sulked. But he's coming over today. We're going bike riding."

"Did you tell Aunt Carol yet?"

"Next question."

"Susie?"

"What?"

"Do you think Jeff went home with that woman?"

There was a long silence. "Dee. You're not going with him. You don't have any right—"

"I know. But it makes me sick. Doesn't he have any taste?"

"Well, he's a grown-up man. He has to . . . they have to . . ."

"So you think he did it?"

"I don't know! She was the one coming on to him. He didn't look one way or the other about it. Why don't you ask him about it, if it bothers you?"

"Are you serious? I couldn't do that!"

"Then forget it. That's my advice."

"I can't forget on command. You going to be out all day?"

"Who knows? I'll call you tomorrow."

"Okay. Bye."

"Bye."

The apartment was very quiet after that. Deidre turned the air up, even though she wasn't hot, just to have some background noise. It was going to be a lonely summer, she decided, if Susie hung around with Curt every day and her mother kept "working late." If only she and Jeff could . . . She looked at the ceiling. She wondered if he was awake yet. She wondered if he'd even come home last night.

Deidre put on shorts and a T-shirt and toweled her hair dry. She could go up there and find out. If no one answered his door, she'd know he had stayed out all night. If he answered the door looking guilty and tried to get rid of her, she'd know someone else was there. But it would be really pushing it to go up there again, wouldn't it? It was starting to look like she was chasing him. He should really make the next move . . . but he couldn't, because of his age. She really had to make all the moves to show him it was all right. Even if he had feelings for her, he might be holding back, thinking she was too young and innocent to understand. She had to let him know what she was ready for.

But she couldn't go up there again! Not without a good excuse, anyway. Why did neighbors visit each other? Lost dog? Locked out? Borrow a cup of sugar?

Forget this, she told herself. *It's crazy. You're crazy. You're just a kid and nothing is ever going to happen with this guy so just forget it.*

She poured herself a glass of orange juice and sat down at the kitchen table to plan the picnic. *Barbecued chicken,* she wrote in her neat, rounded handwriting, *red-pepper potato salad vinaigrette, raspberries and kir, pound cake, chocolate sauce . . .*

Muffins! Perfect. They were fun to make and portable. Years ago she had developed a bran muffin recipe loaded with nutmeg that people always raved about. She hadn't tried it in a while, though. She decided she'd make a practice batch this morning. And just to be sure, she might get someone to test them. . . . Deidre jumped up eagerly and began checking her cupboards, praying all the ingredients were there.

I

Jeff answered the door in a terry-cloth robe, toweling at the back of his head. "Oh, hi!" he said. "What brings *you* here?"

"Did I wake you up?" Deidre asked anxiously.

"No, no. I just came back from the pool. I like to swim in the morning when it's not crowded."

Deidre stored this important information. "Well, have you got a minute? I need an opinion on something."

"Oh, sure!" He stood aside. "Just let me go get dressed. Make yourself at home. What's in the basket?"

The story of Red Riding Hood flashed into Deidre's mind. "It's a surprise. That's what I want your opinion on."

"Okay. Back in a flash." He loped off down the hall to his bedroom. "I love surprises," he added over his shoulder.

Deidre set the basket of muffins on the table and went to the piano to pet Cyril. She tried to keep her mind off what was going on in the other room, but the sound of drawers opening and closing didn't help. "Hello, kitty," she said, touching him gently. He hissed and batted her away.

"Okay!" Jeff called, trotting back down the hall, pulling a green polo shirt over his head. "What's the surprise?" He sat down on the couch to catch his breath and looked up at Deidre with that puppyish expression. Up close he was almost hard to look at. He had a coppery tan that made his eyes look pale and luminous, like green grapes. His hair, still damp, was a streaky, brassy blond. Last night in the darkness of the club he had looked washed out, but here in the daylight he was big and powerful and glowing.

Deidre swallowed several times, trying to remember her speech. "Well, I made some muffins. I'm practicing for a picnic I have to cater this weekend and I need somebody's opinion."

"Oh, boy!" he said. "That's something I'm very good at. Eating. I'm starved too. I haven't had my breakfast or anything. This is great."

Deidre's breath caught. "Really? You haven't eaten yet? Do you . . . want me to make breakfast for you?"

"Oh, no!" he cried. "Oh, God. No. You don't have to do that. You're a guest. I never eat normal meals anymore anyway. Just the muffins are fine."

"No, you don't understand," Deidre said, forgetting to be shy in the passion of the moment. "Cooking is . . . what I do. I love any chance to cook. I'm going to *study* culinary arts. So you see, the opportunity to cook, for me, is like a *treat.*"

"Okay, okay!" He laughed, holding up his hands. "You twisted my arm! But you're not going to find much to work with out there. I'm not very good at buying groceries or any of those other adult skills like balancing checkbooks, maintaining my car, paying income tax . . . If I keep on living alone, I'll probably end up in jail."

You need someone like me, Deidre thought. She said, "Have you got eggs?"

"Yeah."

"If you've got eggs, I can make breakfast."

"Man," he said, shaking his head. "I just must be living right!"

While Deidre broke the eggs into the bowl, Jeff pulled a barstool up to the serving counter, so he could talk to her. She filled a champagne glass with pineapple juice for him to sip on. "I'm really glad you showed up today," he said. "There's something I've been meaning to ask you."

Deidre was at the stove, stirring a panful of onions and mushrooms. She froze in midstir and looked at him. "What?" she said softly.

"It's about my rhapsody. Remember my rhapsody?"

She opened the refrigerator and took out a package of boiled ham and a container of Parmesan cheese. "Yes?"

113

"I finally found a title for it. Your name. *Deidre.* But I thought I should really ask your permission first."

Deidre dropped a spoon on the floor. "My name?" she said.

"Yeah." He took a sip. "Would you be flattered or insulted?"

The vegetables were on the verge of scorching. Deidre quickly grabbed a new spoon and gave them another stir. "Why?" she said. "Why would you want to use my name?"

He tipped his head back to drain the glass. "Because it's such a beautiful name and it just expresses the mood I'm trying to go for. I've been thinking about it ever since I met you. Would you mind?"

Deidre forced herself to be calm and get on with her work. She chopped the ham very deliberately. "No, of course not," she said, just above a whisper. "I'd be very honored."

"Well, don't be." He laughed. "The damn thing will probably never see the light of day. What kind of name is Deidre anyway? Does it mean anything?"

"It's Gaelic," she said. "It means 'sorrow.'"

"Jeez! Who would name a baby 'sorrow'?"

"Irish people, I guess." She shook some cheese into her egg mixture. She wished he had more herbs and spices, but she made do with black pepper. A little garlic and basil and she could have really shown him. "Jeff," she said, "I have a confession to make to you."

"You can't cook and you're faking this whole thing!" he said. "That will break my heart."

"No, I wanted to tell you I went to your club last night. I saw your show. It was absolutely fantastic. You're way too good for that place." She poured the egg mixture over the vegetables and adjusted the flame. For a few minutes she concentrated on cooking, waiting for him to say something. When he didn't, she finally looked up.

He was just staring at her. "You did?"

"Yes." Her stirring hand was a little shaky.

"You came all the way into Fort Lauderdale?"

"I was with some friends."

His expression was unreadable. "What did you do that for?"

Deidre struggled with a blush attack. "Because. I think you're very talented. I wanted to see you work."

He frowned. He almost looked angry. "Why didn't you tell me you were there?"

"I didn't want to bother you."

"You're under eighteen, aren't you?"

He wasn't sure! "Yes. I didn't drink. I just had a Coke with my friends and listened to you." She looked up. "What's the matter? Did I do something wrong?"

More than anything he looked baffled, confused. "No . . . no, of course not. It just makes me feel funny, I guess, that you didn't let me know you were there. I don't know. . . . Well, how did I sound?"

"Like I said. Too good for that place." She divided the

eggs between two of his bone-china dessert plates and took the muffins from the oven where they'd been warming. "You're a very gifted artist, Jeff."

He was really staring holes in her, almost as if seeing her for the first time. "*Thank* you. But look, if you ever do that again, let me know you're there. Okay?"

"Okay. Here. Let's eat this before it gets cold." Deidre gave him his plate and poured him a champagne glass full of coffee. She was amazed at her own composure and lack of embarrassment. She felt elated, in fact, almost powerful. Somehow, she felt, she'd gotten the upper hand.

▌

"God!" said Jeff, pushing his chair back. "You're not kidding. You are a chef. I don't see how you can make something that tastes that good out of the junk in my kitchen. Want to come up here and make my breakfast every day?"

Don't tempt me, Deidre thought. "So the muffins are okay?" she asked, even though she knew. He'd eaten six of them.

"Fantastic. So that's what you want to do for a living? That's really wild."

"I'm going to open my own restaurant someday. In New York or Miami."

"What kind?"

"I can't decide. I like a lot of different things and it will depend on the trends at that time. Like, right now,

Southwestern is going out, Cajun is so far in it's out, Thai is a cliché. I think maybe a New Southern restaurant. New Yorkers would probably like that because they won't know anything about it."

"What's the matter with French?" he said.

"The market is glutted. Plus there's too much saturated fat, unless you do nouvelle cuisine and everybody hates that."

"Too bad," he said. "French is romantic. I always like things that aren't good for me. In fact, that's probably *why* I like them. I gotta have something to rebel against, even if it's my own health and safety. You know? Hey! Want to hear some of your rhapsody? I had a big breakthrough after I started thinking about using your name for the title. I've written a whole new section."

"I would love to hear it," Deidre said.

The telephone rang.

"Aw, shit!" Jeff said. "Excuse me." He had to hunt a minute for the phone, which was under a shirt. "Hello?" Suddenly his whole expression changed. He looked as if he were holding his breath, afraid to move. "Oh. Hi. What do *you* want?"

Deidre thought of the woman from the bar last night. That cow. She picked irritably at her food.

"I'm *fine,*" he said angrily. "How are *you?* Oh, that's great. I can't tell you how happy I am to hear that. Look, I can't talk now, I have company."

Deidre smiled to herself.

"That's none of your business, is it? That's right. Look, you don't need to call and check up on me. I'm a big, grown-up boy."

Deidre got up to clear the table. Maybe it was his mother. It certainly didn't sound like he had a good relationship with her.

"I don't *want* you to care about me!" he shouted so suddenly, Deidre almost dropped their plates. That wasn't his mother. Then she realized. It had to be that old girlfriend from the photograph. Chrissie.

"Well, you see, you just can't have it both ways," he said, shifting to the other ear.

Deidre quietly scraped plates, wondering if she should make some move to go.

"Fine, I told you. Fine. You'd be *surprised.* How about you? Oh, that's too bad. That really breaks my heart, Chris."

Deidre was shocked by his tone. She'd never heard him speak that way before. She'd thought he was the kind of person who never got angry. But he was definitely angry now.

"Look, why don't you just . . ." He looked up and caught Deidre's eye through the pass-through. "Wait a second." He put his hand over the mouthpiece. "Do me a favor?" he asked Deidre.

"You want me to go?" she asked quickly.

"No! I'm going to play for you! Have you got time? I don't want you to go at *all.* But I have to take just a few minutes and finish this up. I think I'd better take it in the bedroom. So would you hang this up for me? I promise it won't be more than five minutes."

"Sure," Deidre said.

"Thanks." To Chrissie he said, "I need to change phones. Hold on." He put the receiver down and stalked down the hall, muttering to himself. "Okay!" he called to Deidre.

She edged toward the telephone as if it were a live wire, waging the worst moral struggle of her life. All she had to do, she knew, was click the receiver and he'd think she'd hung up. She could listen to the whole thing.

"Jeff?" came a strident female voice from the receiver. "Who is that? Who's there with you?"

"I told you. It's none of your *business*!"

Deidre replaced the receiver in its cradle and sat down on the couch. There was too much at stake, she felt, to play silly games. She had seen his eagerness to welcome her in this morning, his look of discomfort and confusion when she told him she'd been to his club. He had eaten her cooking. He had named his rhapsody for her. He had begged her not to go. For the first time she really felt as if this was more than a fantasy or a game. Something was really happening between the two of them. Something special. Deidre folded her hands in her lap and patiently waited her turn.

▮9▮

Deidre had been waiting all week to see what kind of outfit Mr. Maxwell would wear to a picnic. She couldn't picture him in jeans or shorts, but she knew he couldn't possibly show up in one of his Italian suits. It turned out to be stone-colored Dockers and a white knit golf shirt. Somehow in these clothes he looked even more precise and immaculate than before. He had brought a bunch of orchids, which Deidre held on her lap in the car. The scent rising from them mixed deliciously with Mr. Maxwell's cherry cologne. He drove with his right hand only, hanging his left elbow out the window. Deidre, who sat behind him, found herself staring at that clean, strong-looking male arm. He had a trace of sunburn and one lonely freckle above the elbow.

"You want to go to Tradewinds Park or Mullins?" he asked Deidre's mother.

Mrs. Holland was also appealingly overdressed in an

orange sundress with spaghetti straps. "Whichever one you want," she countered.

"Let's go to Tradewinds," he said. "Then, if we want to after lunch, we could go to Butterfly World."

Mrs. Holland glanced at him. "*Butterfly* World!"

He glanced back. "Yeah. Haven't you ever heard about it? They have all these—"

"Yes, I know what it is," she interrupted, laughing nervously, "but you don't have to do something like that just to please us women. Surely you wouldn't want to spend the afternoon looking at butterflies and flowers."

He glanced at her again. "I *grow* flowers!" he reminded her. "I love flowers!"

Mrs. Holland looked out the passenger window and did not answer.

Deidre was as baffled as usual by their interaction. However, today she had more important things on her mind. There was a beautiful, unfinished rhapsody burned into her memory. A rhapsody named for her, inspired by her. *Deidre.* She could still hear every note and chord, exactly as Jeff had played it for her. She knew as long as she lived, she would never forget that hot, still morning in his apartment, the way he looked at the piano, his hair gently stirred by the breeze from the ceiling fan, eyes full of love for the music, fingers caressing the keys. . . . Some of the love he felt for this composition, Deidre knew, was part of what he felt for her. She didn't expect him to talk about it yet. It might be years before they really talked about it. But she knew now it was something Jeff felt as deeply as she did.

She felt sorry for other couples. Susie's whole summer was turning into a struggle with Curt. She called every day with a new episode. All their encounters were alike. They would be getting along fine, then Curt would try something and Susie would stop him and he would either sulk or yell at her and storm off. Then, the next day, he would call and they'd make up and start all over again. Sometimes, listening to Susie tell it, Deidre almost felt Susie was *enjoying* the turmoil.

"Well," Mr. Maxwell said nervously, "why don't we go to Tradewinds, anyway, and when we get there we can decide if it's appropriate for me to like butterflies and flowers."

"You don't need to be sarcastic," Mrs. Holland muttered.

"I just want to know which goddamn *park* to drive to!" he shouted.

Mrs. Holland looked at him coldly. "*You're* the boss," she said.

Deidre felt sorry for them all.

▌

The "boss" decided on Tradewinds, which would have been Deidre's choice anyway. It was bigger than Mullins Park and had a river running through it.

They found a nice little shelter-house and Deidre set an elaborate and beautiful table, featuring Mr. Maxwell's orchids as a centerpiece. The food, of course, was excellent and eating seemed to quiet the grown-ups down and keep them from bickering. Deidre, after compulsively tasting everything, tuned out of their conversation, which was mostly gossip about clients. She picked slowly at a piece of cold chicken, watching a cormorant sun himself on the riverbank and listening to *Deidre* in her head again. She felt warm and drowsy and luxurious. Sunlight sparkled on the river and the air was heavy with the scent of orchids and cherries and Chablis. The piano melody in her mind was beautifully complemented by the soft creak of wind in the palm trees and the gentle clank of silverware.

Deidre finished eating and went to another picnic table, stretching out on the bench and gazing at a wall of cypress trees across the river, whose upper branches were rippling in the wind. She closed her eyes and let the rhapsody lead her into a dream.

A while later she woke up. Lunch had been packed away and Mr. Maxwell was holding her mother's hand and talking softly. They were both still drinking wine. Mr. Maxwell glanced over. "She's awake," he said. As if on command they both got up and came to Deidre's table.

She sat up, yawning, feeling embarrassed. "It must be the heat," she said.

They were both gazing at her fondly. "Your lunch was just wonderful," Mr. Maxwell said. "I really think your cooking is some of the best I've ever tasted."

"Thank you," Deidre said, lowering her eyes. "That's a big compliment coming from you. I know you've eaten in a lot of four-star restaurants."

"I have," he said. "And I appreciate culinary talent. You've really got it. Someday you'll be up there with the best of them."

"*Thank* you," she said, almost breathless. Did he realize how important such a statement was to her? She hoped he wasn't just saying it. Compliments from family and friends were one thing, but from an actual connoisseur . . . "Do you want your dessert now?" she asked. "Or would you like to wait awhile?"

Mr. Maxwell glanced at Deidre's mother. "I'm still pretty full. . . ." he said.

"I was just thinking about taking a nap myself," said Mrs. Holland with a stagy yawn. "Why don't you two take a little walk together and we'll have dessert when you come back?"

"Sounds good to me," said Mr. Maxwell immediately.

It was pitifully obvious they had cooked this up together, probably thinking it was important for Deidre and Mr. Maxwell to *bond* or some such rubbish. But Deidre liked the idea anyway. "Sure," she said, getting up.

They walked along the riverbank in silence. It was afternoon now and so hot, the grass didn't spring back when they stepped on it. It just lay there, defeated. Bright orange dragonflies hovered and darted over the river. The heat was like an embrace.

The silence between them was not strained, but pleasant and comfortable. Mr. Maxwell, like Deidre, did not feel the need to chatter. He spoke only when he had something to say. After a while Deidre noticed they were walking in perfect synchronization. He was wearing expensive-looking sunglasses that gave him a slightly tough appearance. She watched his shadow, moving rhythmically with her own. *This is what it's like to have a father,* she thought.

"Let's sit down," he said. They had reached a sheltered bend in the river, where they were hidden from boaters and other picnickers. She had observed before he had a slight aversion to crowds and strangers.

They sat on the bank, side by side. He flipped his sunglasses up through his fine hair, so Deidre could see his eyes. She had never seen him before without any kind of glasses. He looked very vulnerable. She wondered, for the first time, how old he was. He might actually be younger than her mother. His demeanor made him seem very mature, but across the eyes he looked almost like a kid.

"What's it like to be fourteen?" he asked her. "I forget."

"It's the same as every other year, so far," she replied.

He nodded. "That's why I can't remember, I guess. Actually, I never really *was* fourteen. You know?"

She knew. "I'm not *really* fourteen either."

He smiled. "How old are you? I mean *really.*"

She smiled back. You couldn't play this kind of game with just anybody. "Thirty-five," she said.

"Yeah, that's about right. When I converse with you, you seem about thirty-five."

"How old are you?" she asked shyly.

"You mean my actual age or what we were talking about?"

"What we were talking about."

"Sixty-seven."

"Sixty-seven! Do you really mean you feel like that?"

"Yes! What do you expect? I'm like you. I was thirty-five when I was fourteen. You pay a price for that. Now I'm chronologically thirty-five, but I feel like sixty-seven."

He *was* younger than her mother! Chronologically, at least. "What are you going to feel like when you're sixty-seven?" Deidre asked playfully.

He smiled. "Maybe that's when I'll finally have the guts to be a kid."

She laughed. She really liked him. She found herself memorizing all the details of him: his squarish fingers and short, immaculate fingernails, the strong bridge of his nose, his pale, fine hair. If he became her stepfather, they could talk like this all the time.

"Can I ask you an inappropriate and immoral question?" he said suddenly.

Deidre froze, all her junior-high training coming to her. Stepfathers, baby-sitters, any overly friendly adult—be on your guard! "What?" she said, glancing around to decide where she would run if he grabbed at her.

"Do you think your mom likes me?" he asked.

Deidre relaxed again, feeling foolish. "Sure she does. You guys are going out and everything. She hasn't gone out without anybody since Dad died."

He chose that fascinating moment to drop his sunglasses back down and conceal his eyes. "How long ago was that?" he asked, trying to sound casual.

"Twelve years ago. I was only two."

All she could see was her own reflection in his lenses. "She never dated anybody that whole time?"

Deidre shook her head no. "So you must have something going for you," she joked.

"How do you feel about the whole thing?" he asked.

She looked at the river. "Okay. It's a little weird sometimes, because I think I sort of got the feeling she was never going to date anybody. Ever. I mean, when this first started happening, it was a surprise. I've never seen my mom in this situation."

"It must seem strange for her too," he said thoughtfully. "I mean, she's out of practice. *I* feel that way and my divorce was just last year. But it feels funny, at our age to be, you know, doing the high school stuff."

"Uh-huh," Deidre said. She was quiet on purpose so he would tell more.

"See, the reason I'm asking this is . . ." He broke off and turned toward the river. He was silent so long, Deidre thought he wasn't going to finish his thought, but finally he spoke again. "Sometimes your mom acts kind of . . . funny with me. I mean, she's so hot and cold about it. A lot of the time I feel like I'm really . . . ticking her off. You know? But other times she's perfectly friendly. I know I shouldn't be saying *any* of this to you."

"I won't tell her."

"I know that, but you're her daughter. And you're just a kid. It's horrible for me to dump this stuff on you."

"No, I'm thirty-five, remember?"

He laughed. "Well? What do you think? Does the woman like me or not?"

Deidre laughed at his exasperated tone. "Well, honestly, I don't know. I can't tell either. I mean, it looks the same way to me. Half the time she acts like she likes you, and half the time she seems to be picking a fight."

"Yeah!" he said. "Exactly!"

"But my mom is hard to figure out. She . . . doesn't always say what she means. She doesn't . . . think things through. I think she's probably nervous in a new situation. She's just not used to it."

"I hope it's something like that," he said. "Because I really like her."

Deidre looked at him. "Do you?"

He looked away. "Yeah."

Deidre tossed a few pebbles in the lake, giving him a minute to recover from his embarrassment. The water was very clear and there were spotted carp schooling just under the surface, snapping at the dragonflies.

"I'm glad," Deidre said finally. "Because *I* really like *you.*"

He looked at her, then away. "You want to start calling me Henry or anything?"

"Sure."

He got up abruptly, brushed himself off, and extended a hand. "All right!" he said. "I can't take it anymore! I *saw* that can of Hershey syrup in the hamper and I want to know what you're going to do with it."

She let him help her up. "I put that in just for you," she said.

After that they were both too embarrassed to speak. They went back to the shelter in silence, the same way they'd come.

I

After the cake Deidre decided to give Mr. Maxwell a break and take another walk by herself. She waited a decent interval to see if he was going to suggest Butterfly World again, but he was apparently too scared to do that, so Deidre muttered something about exercise and left them alone.

She walked along the riverbank, pretending Jeff was beside her. After a while she extended her left hand slightly, letting him hold it. The landscape took on a new sparkle now that they were seeing it together. This was the kind of thing they might do someday—walk along a riverbank or a beach, not talking, just sharing time and space. That, she felt, was the most important part of love.

Jeff wanted to sit down in the same place as Mr. Maxwell. Still holding hands, they settled on the riverbank. Silently, Deidre asked Jeff if he was upset, because he had been very quiet. He was moody and complex and needed to be watched. No, he said, he was just sleepy. He lay down and put his head in Deidre's lap. She stroked his hair. The melody began to play again. Deidre felt deliciously peaceful and secure. She felt deep in her soul this would really happen someday. Somehow, she and Jeff would get together.

They stayed that way a long time, enjoying their companionable silence. Finally, Deidre couldn't ignore the low angle of the sun. "It's getting late, love," she said softly. "We have to get back."

Jeff whined, but obediently got up and held out his hand to her. They brushed each other off and walked back, acting silly, swinging hands and bumping into each other.

But when the shelter-house came into view, Deidre let go of Jeff's hand and he melted away to nothing, shoved aside by what she saw. Her mother and Mr. Maxwell were sitting on one of the benches, making out.

Deidre froze and watched, breathing hard. She wanted to look away, but couldn't. All they were doing, really, was kissing, but it was the *way* they were kissing. Like people kiss in the movies when you know they're doing it, even though the camera doesn't go down there. Deidre's mother had pulled Mr. Maxwell's shirt-tail out so she could run her hands over his bare back, and *his* hands were everywhere, crushing up different parts of the orange sundress and caressing. Deidre knew it was crazy to be upset, but it was an upsetting thing to see. She didn't want to see anyone touch her *mother* like that. She didn't want to see her mother touch *anyone* like that. And mixed with the horror there was this almost sinful feeling of excitement that she was getting to *see* such a thing, that they might go farther, do more. She might see a naked man. She might see what sex looked like.

Her body was reacting now. Her breath had become shallow and her heart was beating fast. She felt hot all over. Then, some kind of nausea or panic rose up in her and she turned and ran away as fast as she could, as if something terrible were chasing her.

·10·

Deidre was getting sunburned. For three successive mornings she had come to the pool at nine o'clock, hoping to see Jeff, and three times she'd been disappointed. His exact words had been "I like to swim in the morning when it's not crowded." When she'd gone to his apartment, the morning he played *Deidre* for her, he had just come back from the pool at ten o'clock. So that had to mean he usually swam at nine. So *where was he*? Why did he have to be so inconsistent? Why would he tell her he did something every morning when he really didn't? That was the main thing wrong with humanity, as Deidre saw it. You couldn't depend on any of them to tell the truth.

She applied another layer of Super Shade, to ward off cancer and premature aging. She hoped Jeff appreciated she was risking her very life for a chance to be with him. Yesterday, briefly, she had been tempted to just forget this plan and go up and knock on his door, but that would be the third time. She didn't want to appear calculating.

The security gate clanged and Deidre whipped around anxiously, but it was just Mrs. Arnfeldt from the fifth floor. She wore a tight black bathing cap and a black tank suit with white insets. Deidre couldn't help noticing this gave Mrs. Arnfeldt the exact markings of a killer whale. As she lumbered through the gate, a pig-faced, red-haired ten-year-old boy raced by her, nearly knocking her down in his eagerness to get to the pool. He wore lime-green surfer Jams and carried a large, menacing Boogie board.

"Clay!" Mrs. Arnfeldt shrieked. "Don't run in the pool area!"

"Blow off," Clay muttered, carefully pitching his voice not to carry through the bathing cap. He hurled himself and the board into the deep end with a prodigious splash.

"Hello, Deidre," Mrs. Arnfeldt said, waddling over. "How is your mother?"

It might have been paranoia, but Deidre thought she heard some implied criticism in the question, as if Mrs. Arnfeldt suspected she wasn't a good daughter. "Fine," she said quietly.

"She works so hard," Mrs. Arnfeldt continued. "Poor thing."

"She *likes* her job," Deidre said.

Mrs. Arnfeldt heaved herself into the chair beside Deidre's. "Oh, but it's so hard raising a child without a husband! That's what I keep warning my daughter, whenever she gets fed up. I say, 'Think if you had to raise your family all alone!' I don't mean Clay's mother, I mean my oldest daughter."

Deidre wasn't listening. "Oh," she said. "Clay's your grandson?" She glanced at the splashing frenzy in the deep end.

"Yes." Mrs. Arnfeldt beamed. "He's Cassandra's child. Cassandra's the one who married the Cleveland dentist. Clay likes to come and visit me every summer."

Deidre was fairly sure it was *Florida* Clay liked to visit, but didn't say so. She studied her nails, trying not to get angry. Why had God punished her this way, sending Mrs. Arnfeldt instead of Jeff?

"You're getting sunburned, dear," Mrs. Arnfeldt remarked.

"I know." Deidre sighed.

Clay, meanwhile, was trying to surf in the pool. He paddled his board up to speed, stood up clumsily, and toppled, smacking his rear end on the board before plunging backward into the depths. He bobbed up, choking, clinging to the board and coughing up pints of pool water.

"His father is just like that," Mrs. Arnfeldt said. "Clay! Clay!"

"What? What?" he mocked.

"Get out of the water. I want to introduce you to someone."

God really hates me, Deidre thought.

Clay's reaction was similar. "What? Oh, sh . . ." he grumped, but hauled himself up the pool ladder and sloshed over to them. He glared at Deidre, wiping his nose with the back of his hand.

"This is Deidre Holland," Mrs. Arnfeldt explained. "The one whose father died."

What a great thing to be known for, Deidre thought. She wondered if poor Clay had been told the personal problems of everyone in the building.

However, this note of pathos slowed down the momentum of Clay's malice. He could hardly be rude to a bereaved person. "Sorry," he muttered.

"It's okay," Deidre said, trying not to laugh.

Clay raised pleading eyes to his grandmother. "Can I get back in the water?"

"Yes, you may," she said.

He gave Deidre a sort of smile, pivoted, ran to the deep end, screamed, and dived, splaying his legs like a frog.

"He's going to break a lot of hearts someday," said Mrs. Arnfeldt.

Before Deidre could comment, the gate clanged again. She turned and there he was, her reward from God, Jeff in living color, which today meant a pair of madras trunks and a beach towel featuring Tony the Tiger. Catching her eye, he broke into a delighted smile. "Hey!" he called.

"Hi!" she said shrilly.

He slung the towel over one shoulder and came to

them. "Hi, there, Dixie!" He grinned at Mrs. Arnfeldt. "How are you today?"

"Oh, you know me!" She smiled. "I never complain!"

Deidre was speechless, not just that Mrs. Arnfeldt's first name was Dixie, but that she and Jeff were so chummy.

He sat down on the other side of Mrs. Arnfeldt and kicked off his flip-flops. "I lucked out, didn't I?" he asked them. "All the beautiful women are here and I'm the only man!"

"Oh, no you're not!" Mrs. Arnfeldt trumpeted in a schoolgirl voice. "My grandson Clay is here!" She pointed proudly to a pair of white feet sticking up out of the water.

"Handsome boy!" Jeff remarked, winking at Deidre. "Is that Cassandra's son?"

"That's right."

Deidre felt oddly jealous. Of course it was silly, but she wanted to be his only friend in the building. She supposed it made sense, if he and Mrs. Arnfeldt always swam in the mornings, that they had struck up this acquaintance. Jeff made friends with anyone in his vicinity. Certainly Mrs. Arnfeldt was nothing to be jealous of, but still . . .

"Hey, you're getting a sunburn there, kid!" Jeff told Deidre.

Kid! "I know it!" she snapped, wishing she could tell him it was all his fault.

"Clay?" Mrs. Arnfeldt called. "Are you ready to get out?"

Clay was experimenting with the laws of physics, holding his board underwater and feeling it resist. "No," he said flatly.

You little . . . Deidre thought. Her curse was powerful. The board shot through Clay's fingers and belted him under the jaw. He screamed in pain and went under.

Jeff was up like a spaniel, ready to help. Mrs. Arnfeldt struggled with her chair.

But Clay surfaced and pulled himself onto the board, fighting back tears. "That hurt!" he proclaimed.

"Come here, man," Jeff said with authority. "Let me look at you. I used to be a lifeguard."

Clay looked at Jeff with reverence. He paddled to the side and pulled himself out, sloshing to Jeff. Jeff held his chin and tilted his head this way and that, examining. "You need to ice it, pal," he said. "Otherwise, you'll get a bruise. Don't try to swim the rest of the day. You're okay and everything, but your judgment might be impaired. You can swim tomorrow if you want to."

Clay gazed at Jeff as if a god were speaking. "Thanks, man," he said. "Come on, Grandma! We have to *ice* it!"

"All right, all right," she squawked, struggling to her feet, flustered at this damage to a child in her care.

"He'll be fine," Jeff told her. "He's made of iron. Just put ice on it for a half hour and don't let him tear around."

"Thank you," said Mrs. Arnfeldt. She and Clay walked away solemnly, casting backward glances at their hero.

Jeff watched them go, then turned to Deidre, his eyes crinkled with amusement. "I thought we'd *never* be alone!" he said theatrically.

Deidre felt the blood rush to her face. He was kidding, but was he also serious? Maybe he had made up all that stuff about icing it just to get rid of them! Was that too much to hope for? "It seems like forever since I've seen you," she said quietly.

"Really? You were just over the other day!"

"It was last Friday. When you played the rhapsody for me."

"Oh, yeah! Well, that's why you haven't seen me. I've been really working on that. Ever since I gave it your name, everything just clicked into place. I've been writing up a storm. I think I'll have it finished pretty soon."

"I've been hearing parts of it through the ceiling," she said. "It's beautiful."

"Thank you. When it's done you can come up for the premiere."

"I'd love to. Then what happens?"

"Pardon?"

"When you finish a musical composition, what do you do with it? Where do you send it?"

He laughed. "I don't know! I've never finished a musical composition before. You have to do something to

get it copyrighted or published or something, I guess.
. . . I don't know what the hell happens to classical
music, I mean to get it *played*. I just figured I'd put it in
a closet and they'll find it when I die."

"Then you wouldn't get royalties."

"I don't think you get much the other way either.
Want to go in?"

"What?"

"I want to swim. You want to go in with me?"

"Oh, yes!" she cried, jumping up.

"Last one in has to talk to Mrs. Arnfeldt!" he said,
sprinting toward the deep end. He dived in with the
same grace and enthusiasm as Clay.

Deidre sedately used the ladder. Something strange
came over her as soon as she was in the pool. There was
something extremely seductive about being in the water with him. The breeze had died down and the air
around them was still. She swam slowly toward him,
conscious of the lap of water and the soft sparkle of
sunlight all around.

He had propped himself in the corner, putting his
elbows on the sides. When it was wet, his hair took on a
brassy tone and the curl disappeared, giving him a
harder, more masculine appearance. Water glistened
on his shoulders and chest. He grinned at Deidre, then
jackknifed sideways and began to swim the length of
the pool. He used a sidestroke that cut into the water
without making splashes, pulling himself with strong,
even arm strokes.

She watched him and then followed, hurrying until they were parallel and then carefully copying and matching his technique, so they were traveling in perfect rhythm. After a few moments she realized she was experiencing a kind of high. Her whole body felt good from the exertion, and being with Jeff seemed to drive out a kind of tension she lived with most of the time. It was a perfect moment, the surroundings so beautiful, the mood so simple and playful—nothing but splash and sparkle. Then a gust of wind blew and showered the poolside with pink oleander petals. Some of them fell in the water and Deidre swam through them luxuriously, like an Egyptian princess in a rose-scented bath.

They went on that way until they were tired and then Jeff went back to his corner, propping himself up again, kicking his feet like a little boy. Deidre swam to him and stopped a few feet away, holding on to the ladder.

"You're a good swimmer," he said.

"Yes," she agreed modestly. "So are you."

"I love water," he said, throwing back his head and looking up at the sky.

"So do I," she said softly. She drifted closer to him, staring at his chest and the hollow of his throat, imagining what his wet skin would feel like. She slowly put her hand up out of the water. He looked down so suddenly, she jumped back, startled and ashamed.

"You know what's the best thing about water?" he asked.

Deidre was suffering an embarrassing physical reaction to her recent thoughts and not paying attention. "What?" she said.

"It's really good for . . . sneak attacks!" he cried, and splashed a huge wave into her face.

For just a second she was furious, but the sight of him laughing made her happy all over again. "You pig!" she shrieked, splashing him back. They had a frenzied water fight and he grabbed her and held her briefly under the water. When he let her up he cringed, waiting for retaliation, but instead she moved away and pulled herself up on the ladder, gasping.

"I'm sorry!" he cried. "Did I keep you under too long?"

"It's all right," she said. She wasn't drowning. She was breathless. It was the first time they'd ever touched.

Later, they napped together in deck chairs. "Boy," he muttered. "I wish I had something to drink."

"Mmm," Deidre said, almost too contented to form words. "Coke machine over there."

"I don't got no money, honey," he replied. "Anyway, I don't like soda. No, what I have to do is haul my lazy . . . physique out of this chair and go up and get my pineapple juice."

An idea blazed across Deidre's mind like a comet. Happiness had made her brilliant. "Let me run up and get it for you," she said. She got up to help force the issue.

"No! No!" he said. "You don't have to fetch and carry for me. That's terrible. Or do you think I'm too old to take the stairs after exertion?"

"I just want to do it." She held out her hand. "Give me your key."

"It's under the mat," he said.

She was horrified. "You shouldn't do that! That's not safe!"

"I have to! I forget my keys all the time. I'd be locked out every day! Anyway, thieves don't look there anymore because everyone's too smart to do it. Look, I'm awake now. Let me go up. I feel like I'm taking advantage of your sweet nature."

"That's what I want you to do," she assured him. "Look, you get me a Coke from the machine while I'm gone. Then we'll be even." She shoved two quarters into his hand.

"You're too nice to live," he said. "You must be some kind of angel."

Deidre smiled modestly and took flight before he could change his mind.

The elevator took forever. She stamped her feet like an impatient pony, wishing she'd taken the stairs. When she arrived at his door, the full impact of her conquest struck her. She not only had the chance to snoop in his apartment now . . . if he kept the key under the mat, she could go in there anytime he was away!

Heart pounding, she stooped and ceremoniously turned back the corner of the welcome mat. There it was, golden and perfect, like the Holy Grail. She fitted it snugly in the lock and gave a smart turn of the wrist. And the treasure room sprang open.

The dryer was humming away as she walked through the shadowy hall. Cyril had just finished burying something in his sandbox and he scuttled away into the living room, glaring over his shoulder at the intruder.

Time was limited. Jeff was scatterbrained, but she knew it wouldn't take twenty minutes to fix pineapple juice. She had to pick her shot. His desk? Or his bedroom? The bedroom drew her like a magnet.

His messiness, under some control in the rest of the place, ran rampant here. This was where the poster of Paris had ended up, taped crookedly over the bed. The floor was strewn with clothes and shoes, magazines and newspapers. On the nightstand was a champagne glass with dregs of coffee and milk in the bottom, a lamp made to look like a Hollywood studio light, an empty Kleenex box, the telephone and answering machine, and a paperback novel called *In Watermelon Sugar,* which Deidre assumed was a children's book.

The bed was unmade, of course, and had a bright blue spread and blue-striped sheets. Deidre sat down on the bed, picked up a pillow, and hugged it, breathing in deeply. It smelled like sea breezes and laundry detergent, with a faint honey-and-lime scent that was Jeff's. She lay back for just a minute, looking at the ceiling Jeff looked at when he was in bed.

Mindful of time, she forced herself to get up and look at the dresser. The dresser top was very cluttered. The framed photographs of Cyril and Jimmy Buffett were here, but not Chrissie. Good. There was also a model sailboat, a bottle of suntan lotion, *three* gold cuff links, his plastic watch, a comb with one curly blond hair in it, the manual for operating his VCR, a bottle of over-the-counter sleep aids, matches from the Holiday Inn, an empty beer can, a package of tropical-flavored Skittles, a bloody styptic pencil, a flea collar, and a large bottle of cologne, which turned out to be Brut. Deidre unscrewed the top and filled her lungs with the piercing chartreuse scent.

Hurrying now, she inspected the drawers. Socks, all cotton, not mated, whites and brights. Jockey briefs, every color of the rainbow, and one pair of silk paisley boxers that *had* to be a present from Chrissie. Terry bathrobe, crayon-colored sweaters. An array of gaudy beachwear and towels. No undershirts. No pajamas.

The telephone rang. Deidre screamed like a thief who trips a security alarm. The answering machine was on, but Deidre's brilliance was still operating on full. She picked up the phone and said *hello* in the most seductive voice she could muster.

The other party disconnected noisily. "Take that, bitch!" Deidre laughed. She hoped it was Chrissie.

Now she was running late. She wished there were time for the bathroom and the medicine cabinet, but that might take just long enough to make him suspicious. She hurried back to the kitchen, glancing at Cyril, who was quivering with rage at her presumption.

She hurriedly took the can of pineapple juice from the refrigerator. There was another blast of sound and she screamed and nearly dropped the juice on her foot. This time it was the dryer signal.

"Shut up!" she shouted. Her nerves were frayed. She decided she'd better look and see if there were any shirts that needed hanging up. Otherwise, wrinkles would set in.

But it was a load of whites—towels and socks. She pulled out an armload and buried her face in them, nuzzling. One sock fell to the floor. It occurred to Deidre that Jeff had so many socks and was so absent-minded, he'd never know if one was missing. As soon as she thought of it, the idea began to obsess her. She had to have that sock! She put it on her hand like a puppet and rubbed her cheek. It would be so wonderful to have something like this of his, to touch anytime she wanted to.

The rest of the morning, while they talked, she put her hand into the pocket of her cover-up from time to time, secretly touching the soft cotton with a mixture of guilt and excitement like nothing she'd ever felt before.

·11·

Deidre lay supine and limp in the hall, dressed in shorts, a tank top, and Jeff's white tennis sock, staring up at the smoke alarm but not seeing it, seeing only the music that seeped through the ceiling and showered over her like blossoms. *Deidre* was nearly finished. He was working on the final chords, stopping and starting as he experimented. Sometimes the music made colors in the air: aqua and violet and deep, dark blue. It was a sad composition, not really fitting Jeff's definition of rhapsody at all. Strange that someone like Jeff, who was so breezy and upbeat, would uncover this sad melody.

He stopped playing and Deidre rolled over, released from the spell. Her apartment was hot and stuffy at that hour. She lifted the hair from the back of her neck, listening absently for footsteps upstairs, or any other indication of what he might be doing. It was time for him to get ready for work. Sometimes she could hear the water pipes when he took his shower.

Resting her cheek on her elbow, she thought vaguely of dinner. She had chicken thawed out, a fail-safe option. She could do any one of a thousand things. She considered orange sauce. She could brown the chicken and deglaze the pan with orange juice and marmalade. . . .

The telephone rang. She jumped up and ran to it, eager to talk. She had been alone all day. There was always an outside chance, she felt, that Jeff might call someday. *"Have you got a minute?"* he would say. *"I just need somebody to talk to."*

"Hello?" she said breathlessly.

"Hi, honey," said her mother. "What's the matter? You sound like you've been running."

"I've been exercising," Deidre said, which was almost funny because she hadn't moved in the last three hours.

"That's good," her mother said absently. "Listen . . . I . . . Mr. Maxwell wants to have dinner with me tonight."

The chicken *à l'orange* changed in Deidre's mind to a bologna sandwich. "Okay," she said tolerantly.

There was silence on the other end of the phone.

"Mom?"

Mrs. Holland cleared her throat. "Yes. Well. It's kind of a *working* dinner, I guess. We're going to his house and eat Chinese food. . . ."

"I can live with that," Deidre said.

"Well . . . well, honey, I guess we should have discussed this before now. Face-to-face, I mean. I mean, this isn't something to talk about over the phone. . . ."

"Chinese food?"

"No. I don't even know how to say this. I probably shouldn't . . . well, you know Mr. Maxwell and I like each other a lot. . . ."

"Yes." Deidre's stomach was tight, as if braced to take a punch.

"Well . . . would you be upset if I didn't come home tonight?" Mrs. Holland sounded like a guilty child.

"Of course not," Deidre managed, after a second.

Her mother exhaled noisily. "Oh, good. Oh, thank goodness. Because if you would find it even the tiniest bit upsetting . . ."

"I'm a big girl, Mom," Deidre said tonelessly. "Don't worry about me."

"Oh, good. Well . . . I guess I'll call you . . . tomorrow."

"Okay."

"I want you to know this whole situation is driving me crazy."

"Love makes the world go around," Deidre said quietly.

"I wish it didn't. Okay, well . . . will you be all right by yourself? His number is in my address book and if you have any—"

"I'm a big girl," Deidre repeated. "Don't worry."

"That's impossible. Promise me you'll call if—"

"Good-bye, Mom."

"Okay. All right. I love you."

"I love you too." Deidre politely waited until her mother disconnected before slamming the phone down. *What am I angry about?* she asked herself. She wanted her mother to be happy. She liked Mr. Maxwell. She didn't object on any moral grounds. Maybe it was just the idea of being alone all night. That must be it. She just wasn't used to it. She lifted the receiver again and hung it up gently to show there were no hard feelings.

Hugging herself, she drifted into the living room. The sun was going down, slanting in the front window in narrow shafts, like orange spears. She turned the air conditioning down a notch. It was seven-fifteen. She should eat something. But her stomach felt tight. Jeff would be leaving for work about now.

The orange light dimmed and vanished. She pulled up Jeff's sock and walked mechanically around the apartment, pulling drapes and turning on lamps. She double-checked the front door to see if it was locked and bolted. Everything was so still. She knew she should play a tape or turn on the TV or something. She accused herself of deliberately keeping the apartment quiet so she could feel sorry for herself. *You go in the kitchen and eat something,* she commanded.

The kitchen lights sprang on, almost hurting her eyes. Deidre opened the refrigerator. As always, she found refuge in the coolness and the array of food, like a palette of paints waiting to be mixed. But when it was just for herself, her imagination wouldn't spark. She forced down a dry peanut-butter sandwich and a glass of milk, sitting at the kitchen table, listening to the clock tick.

In desperation she went back to the telephone.

"Hello?" It was Sondra, trying to sound sophisticated.

"Hi. It's Deidre. Is Susie there?"

"Deidre?" Sondra said poisonously. "I thought Susie was supposed to be with *you!*"

Oh, God. Oh, no. What a slipup. Usually, she was more careful. "She *is* supposed to be with me," Deidre said haltingly. "That's why I'm calling. What time did she leave?"

Sondra yawned. "Oh, I don't know. Just about five minutes ago, I guess."

Thank you, God, Deidre thought sincerely. "Oh, okay. Oh, there's someone at the door now. Thanks."

"Yeah." Sondra hung up loudly.

That was close. Susie would have killed her if Sondra had been tipped off. Deidre sighed. "Everybody's got a date but me," she said. Then, in the easy, effortless way miracles always happen, a thought slipped into her mind. She looked at the clock. *Why not?* she asked herself. She tried to imagine anything that might be wrong with her idea, any way it could blow up in her face. No! No! There was no way she could get caught. And the rewards . . . She ran to her room, to count out bus fare and choose a dress.

I

Luckily, it was a different waitress. Deidre intended to use a different story. This girl looked like all the other girls except she had a very turned-up nose. Her hair, however, was indistinguishable from that of Nicki the bartender and all the other waitresses. Deidre pictured a box of Miss Clairol labeled BARMAID BLOND. According to her badge this one was Brandy B. She spotted Deidre and walked over slowly, making up her mind how to handle the confrontation.

"You're in the wrong place, honey," she said. "This is the *bar*."

"I know," Deidre said calmly. "Jeff Elliot is my brother."

Brandy B. hadn't expected this. She had to pause to reconsider. "Yeah?"

"Yes. I'm visiting from Gainesville. He invited me to see the show. *He* said it would be okay." Deidre smiled a little. She felt confident. She knew enough about Jeff to pass scrutiny. His family *did* come from Gainesville and he *did* have a little sister.

"You're Beth," said Brandy B.

"That's right." Deidre forced a smile. She was instantly jealous that this girl knew any personal things about Jeff.

"He should have said something! He's crazy about you!" said the waitress, slumping into a relaxed stance.

The test had been passed. "He's always saying how much he misses you."

"Yeah. We're close. So it's okay if I sit here and watch the show?"

"Oh, sure. I mean, I can't serve you alcohol. . . ."

"Oh, no! I just want a Coke."

"No problem. Hey, don't you want a better seat? Close to the stage? There's plenty of tables."

"No! I mean, Jeff gets nervous when he sees people he knows in the audience. He didn't even want to know which night I was coming. So it's better if I stay back here."

"Hey, that's right! I remember Chrissie always used to sit in the back."

Deidre ground her teeth.

"Is that really over?" Brandy B. asked in a lower tone. "I mean, are they really finished?"

"Yes," Deidre said. "Absolutely."

"Well, good! Because the rest of us would like a shot at him! He's too good to be out of circulation. . . . Hey! Tell him I was nice to you. Maybe he'll finally notice I'm alive."

"You bet," Deidre said.

"I'll get your Coke."

You do that, you whore! Deidre thought. She watched Brandy B.'s hip-swinging retreat with disgust. Jeff really ought to work in a classier place. He'd never straighten himself out with all these bimbos around.

When the Coke order went in, Nicki the bartender

glanced at Deidre, but simply nodded to Brandy's remarks. But she did remember Deidre from the other night because she put a lime wedge in the Coke, just as before. This time, without Curt to yell at her, Deidre sucked on it, savoring the flavor that was so much like Jeff's cologne.

It was almost time for the show. Deidre relaxed and sipped, slipping into the fantasy that she was Jeff's girl-friend and, like Chrissie, came here often to see the show. She knew she looked good tonight, in her dark blue dress and sandals. She had braided her hair and wore gold hoop earrings. She was sure she looked at least seventeen.

The spotlight hit the stage. Deidre jumped, and had to struggle to keep her breathing even. Then, there he was, in a cream-colored shirt and pants and a dark blue jacket—very conservative for him. Deidre liked the effect. It was good to know he had some clothes that didn't come from surf shops.

"Thank you," he said to the pitifully thin applause. His mood seemed as toned down as his outfit. Tonight he didn't make any jokes or try to establish rapport with the audience. He just sat down and played "Every Time You Go Away." Deidre wondered if something was bothering him. And just for a second she dared to imagine it had something to do with her.

■

By ten forty-five Deidre had ordered six Cokes and was down to the money she needed for bus fare home. She was seriously worried about Jeff. His performance was adequate, but listless, and between sets he was drinking heavily. The other night he'd had one beer between each set, which he sipped slowly. But tonight he was drinking something in a highball glass and he would tip his head back and drain it straight off, then ask for another. Now, during his last set, he was mumbling his lyrics and faking the accompaniment, just playing chords instead of the melody.

The crowd, which was fairly heavy, was slightly impatient with him. "Speak up!" a man yelled.

Jeff said something back, which, happily, the microphone didn't pick up. Deidre was glad the show was almost over.

For his final number he played an elaborate instrumental version of "Silent Night," stood up shakily, cupped the microphone, and slurred, "Merry Christmas, ladies and gentlemen," before staggering off the stage. There was a mixture of applause and boos, followed by murmurs of confusion.

Jeff went straight to the bar, where Nicki had a fresh drink ready for him. He spoke to her at length, possibly apologizing or explaining himself, and she patted him on the arm. He propped his chin on his fist and sipped morosely.

Deidre didn't know what to do. Every impulse in her body told her to go to him and try to help. But she also knew this was an adult situation she didn't know how to handle. How could she explain her presence there? He'd gotten almost angry before, when he'd found out she came to the show. But on the other hand, he'd said, "Let me know when you're there." So maybe she should do that right now.

He was turned so she looked at his profile. She thought she had never seen a sadder expression in her life. His hand groped around, searching for the drink he'd set down. He was too out of it to look. He picked it up by the rim and drank awkwardly around his fingers. A new thought came to Deidre. If he was that loaded, he shouldn't drive home. It was almost her duty to get him to take a cab. Of course, he had other friends here who could do the same for him. . . .

That settled it. Deidre stood up and marched over. The barstool was a little high for her, but she hoisted herself up with some dignity. Jeff never reacted or changed expression much, he just widened his eyes, as if trying to decide if he was hallucinating.

"Hi," Deidre said.

"Hi," he said cautiously.

Nicki came over. "Want another Coke?"

"No, thanks," Deidre said tensely.

"What did you think of your brother's show?"

"Oh, it was great," Deidre said in a shrill voice. She felt as if she were walking to the edge of a high diving board.

"Who?" Jeff asked, bewildered.

"He's usually a lot better," Nicki said. "Tonight he's being kind of a bad boy." She picked up his hand and slapped it gently to illustrate. "I think he should have his car keys taken away for punishment." She winked at Deidre.

"I agree," Deidre said.

"You've got a good sister," Nicki said to Jeff. "You do what she tells you."

"Huh?" he said.

Nicki smiled at Deidre and moved away.

"Hey!" Jeff said. "She *hit* me! And what's she talking about my *sister* for?"

"Shhh!" Deidre said. "She thinks I'm your sister."

He blinked. "Why?"

"Because that's what I told my waitress. To get in here."

"Ah!" he said. Then he giggled. "You shoulda said, 'I'm with the band.' " Deidre had no idea why, but he seemed to find this hysterically funny. He almost fell off the stool, laughing.

"Calm down!" Deidre said. "Look, have you got any money?"

"Money?" he said. "What for? We gonna go dancing?"

"No. I'm going to call us a cab so we can both get home safely."

"No, no!" he said, shaking his head. "I'm not drunk. I can drive. I'll drive you home. Hey! What are you doing here, anyway?"

"I told you. I came to see you." She looked at his trouser pockets, trying to locate a bulge that looked like car keys.

"Oh," he said. "Off night. Too bad you had to come all the way for that." He touched his forehead as if he were dizzy.

"That doesn't matter," Deidre said. "Give me your wallet and your car keys."

"No! No! No!" He shook his head vigorously. "I'm all right." Softly, he began to sing the Kenny Loggins song of the same name.

Deidre sighed and plunged in, ransacking his pockets.

"Hey!" He giggled. "Stop it! Help! I'm being robbed!"

Nicki and several patrons looked over at Deidre, who got what she wanted but was blushing so hard, it felt like fever. Everyone saw the situation for what it was and turned away.

"Give that stuff back now," he said. "I'm not playing."

"I'm not playing either. I'm going to go call us a cab."

"Boy, I thought you were so sweet. You're a bitch!"

"You'll thank me later on," Deidre said in a shaky voice. She felt like crying, but she was determined to stay calm and responsible.

Jeff slumped over the bar. "Will *not*!" he muttered.

He was still in a bad mood when she loaded him into the taxi. "This is my sister *Beth*," he said to the driver. "She's a *bitch*."

"Where we going?" the driver asked, wearily.

"Seventeen thirty-two Royal Palm in Coral Springs," Deidre said. She wondered if Jeff was being sarcastic or if he was actually confusing her with his sister.

"Take *her* there," Jeff said. "I'm going to Yesterday's. The night is young."

The driver glanced at Deidre sympathetically. "Well, let's take your sister home *first*," he said.

"My destination is closer!" Jeff cried indignantly.

The driver ignored him and headed for Coral Springs.

Jeff used the time to take a nap, slumping against the seat. Unconscious, he looked almost painfully sweet and vulnerable. Deidre wanted to put her arms around him. A lock of hair had fallen across his closed eyes and she brushed it back.

"If he's getting ready to puke, tell me!" the driver called. "I just had the upholstery cleaned in here!"

"Okay," Deidre said.

"He do this all the time?"

Deidre wondered that herself. "No. He's just upset. He broke up with his girlfriend."

"Aw, that's rough," the driver agreed. "I was divorced nineteen months ago." He talked about himself the rest of the way.

"You need help getting him upstairs?" the driver asked as they pulled into the parking lot.

"I'm not sure. Let me see. Jeff?" She touched his face gently. "We're home. Can you walk?"

He opened his eyes, looking confused, then ashamed. "Sure," he said in a soft voice. "How much do I owe you?" he asked the driver.

"Eighteen eighty-six."

"I've got your wallet," Deidre said. "I'll pay him."

"Okay." He got out and walked rapidly away.

Deidre counted out the fare and added what she hoped was a decent tip and scurried after him, carrying his jacket.

He was by the elevators, leaning against the wall with one arm over his eyes. "God, what you must think of me," he whispered.

"No, it's okay." She touched his arm. "Here's the elevator."

He had to hold the handrail inside the elevator car to stay upright. "Jesus!" he said. "You must be in trouble. It's so late. Go on home. I've probably gotten you in trouble."

"No, it's okay. My mother's out for the whole night. That's why I went to the club. I don't have to be any-where." Her heart had begun to beat fast as she real-ized this and what it implied.

He leaned against the hallway while Deidre un-locked his front door. She went in first, laying his blazer and wallet and key ring on the desk in the living room. He came in slowly behind her. Cyril padded in from the kitchen and regarded them both with suspicion.

"You can go now," Jeff said, sinking into the couch. "I'm really okay. I just want to sleep." But he didn't look sleepy. He was gazing numbly at the wall. It wasn't like him not to make eye contact.

"Jeff . . ." she said, "what's the matter? What did you do this for?"

He shrugged.

"If you have a drinking problem, there are places . . ."

"I don't," he said. "I haven't done anything like that for years. I just . . . some stuff is coming to a head and I was feeling sorry for myself. That's all. Look, get out of here. I'm a big boy. You've done too much already."

She still didn't move. "What if I made some coffee and we talked?" she asked.

He didn't speak for a long time. His eyes moved back and forth, as if he were scanning the carpet for something. Finally, when he raised his eyes to her they held the faintest sparkle of tears. "Okay," he said hoarsely.

■

"I don't think you can really understand," he said, cradling his coffee cup. "You're too young."

"I'm not a little kid," she said. "Eat." She had made English muffins to go with the coffee, thickly buttered and honeyed. Jeff loved honey, even put it on his cereal. He bought the kind that comes in a plastic bear. She set the food on the coffee table in front of him and sat on his rocking horse.

He obediently crunched into a muffin. "I guess it's because I have a birthday coming up."

"Really? When?"

"Next week. Next Friday. And . . . at my age a birthday is kind of when you take stock, you know? You think about where you're at. And this year I'm nowhere."

"What are you talking about?" Deidre said, rocking slightly. "You're doing great."

"Oh, but there's a few little things wrong," he said, taking another bite. "My girlfriend left me, my career is a total embarrassment, I don't really have anything to live for except that a *cat* is depending on me. Just petty stuff like that."

"You shouldn't talk that way."

"Why not? I'm thinking that way and you asked. You think I got this drunk because I'm so *happy*?"

Deidre stopped rocking. "How old are you going to be?"

He looked down. "Twenty-six."

He was older than she'd guessed. But she knew that would be a bad thing to say. "Jeff, you're still young. You have to give all this stuff time. A lot of people can't get *any* job in show business."

"A lot of people in show business are millionaires at eighteen! Some of them retire at my age! If I was ever going to really make it, it would have happened by now. Chrissie was right about me. That's why I'm so unhappy. I want a lot of stuff I'm never going to get."

"No!" Deidre said fiercely. "That's not true! Chrissie was wrong! She didn't understand you! You have a lot of

161

talent, Jeff! A lot! That rhapsody is the most beautiful thing I've ever heard. You play *very* well. The only way you can fail is if you quit."

He put his coffee cup down, smiling faintly. "I get it," he said. "This is one of those Frank Capra movies. You're an angel they sent to straighten me out. I've suspected all along you aren't real."

Deidre wondered what on earth that meant. "I'm not an angel," she said. "I'm just . . . your friend."

He smiled warmly. "You're a good one too! You saved my life tonight. But come on! How is it that you pop up whenever I'm about to screw up? You don't think that's divine intervention?"

Deidre shrugged modestly. His praise made her bold. "There's something else I want to say. About Christine. You'll find somebody else someday."

His eyes unfocused. He stared into space a long time. Then he slowly shook his head. "I can't imagine that," he said. "I can't imagine myself with anyone but her." For a second he looked as if he might cry.

Deidre waited carefully until she was sure he was okay. "You just need to be patient. About your career and . . . everything else. You have to give it time. You know what they say about if something's worth having it's worth waiting for?"

He looked at her. "I don't see how somebody your age can have everything so figured out."

She fell back on Mr. Maxwell's theory. "I'm really a thirty-five-year-old in disguise."

"I believe that. And I think I'm a *six*-year-old in disguise."

"I can believe that after tonight!"

"I'm really sorry. That was just awful. You don't know how ashamed I am."

"I'll forgive you if you promise not to do it anymore."

He saluted. "Yes, Guardian Angel. Listen, go home and go to bed. You've earned your Girl Scout badge and then some, and I'm just fine now. Really."

"You want anything else to eat? A sandwich or—"

"No! Really. I need some sleep."

"Okay." She stood up, absently patting the horse's neck. "Good night."

"Good night." He sank into sleep right away, his breathing slowly deepening like that of a kitten or puppy who plays until he's exhausted.

Deidre watched him a few seconds, then stooped and gently brushed her lips against his. His mouth was very warm.

"Oh, sweetheart . . ." he murmured.

She didn't sleep at all that night.

·12·

"Deidre?"

Deidre counted to ten, just to make her wait. "I'm here."

Her mother's footsteps came slowly down the hall. She walked into Deidre's room carrying her briefcase, wearing yesterday's dress. "Hi."

Deidre wove her fingers together. "Hi."

"What's for dinner?"

"I didn't make anything."

Her mother set the briefcase down and sat on the edge of the bed. She moved slowly, like a mammal in the presence of a snake. "I told you I'd be home," she said softly.

Deidre made the church-and-steeple with her hands. "I know. Can't I have a night off once in a while? I don't feel like cooking."

"Sure. You just want to call a pizza or something?"

"You'd have to eat most of it. I'm not very hungry."

"You're angry with me."

Deidre sat up. "No, I'm not."

"It's all right if you are. We can talk it out."

"But I'm not, Mom. I'm not going to pretend to be angry just so we can have a talk."

"Did you do all right by yourself last night?"

"Sure."

"Did you eat anything?"

"I can't remember. Why are you so obsessed with food?"

"I'm not." Her mother looked away.

There was an uncomfortable silence.

Deidre sighed. "I don't know what I should say. Am I supposed to ask you if you had a good time last night?"

Her mother half laughed. "How should I know?"

For the first time in the conversation Deidre met her mother's eyes. "Did you?"

"Sure." Another uneasy laugh. "Look, baby, if you have a problem with this, I can tell him to forget it. You're a whole lot more important than . . . anything."

Deidre picked angrily at her nail polish. "Did I *say* I have a problem with him?"

"No, but—"

"Maybe I've got other things bothering me. How would you know? I don't sit up night and day thinking about you and Mr. Maxwell."

"No, of course—"

"As a matter of fact, I like Mr. Maxwell. If you married him—"

"Oh, honey, nobody's talking about anything like that!"

"Well . . . anyway, I like him. So don't worry."

"Then something else is bothering you?"

Deidre sighed. "Can't I just be a little *down*? Does it have to be some issue that has to be *discussed*? I think it's close to my period."

Her mother exhaled with relief. "Oh, good. I mean, I know how that is. I had something else I wanted to discuss with you, but if it's a bad time . . ."

Deidre laughed listlessly. "No, if it's bad news you might as well give it to me now, while I'm in a crummy mood."

Now Mrs. Holland began to play with *her* fingers. "It isn't bad news, it's just—" She looked up suddenly. "I just hope you know that all this . . . these changes are as upsetting to me as they are to you. Ever since your father died, right up until now, I didn't realize how *easy* I had it. You know? All I had to do was grieve and be depressed. I didn't feel good, but it was easy. Now I'm dealing with a *person,* and it makes everything so complicated."

"Yeah," Deidre said softly. "I guess that's right."

"And things have changed since I was your age. There aren't any *rules*. I don't know . . ."

"What's the matter?" Deidre asked.

"Well . . . I feel weird enough about last night. But . . . he wants me to go away for the weekend."

Deidre imagined two days and two nights of that crushing silence. "When?"

"Next weekend. He wants to drive over to Sarasota. There's a place he used to stay . . . with his wife. He says it's beautiful."

"Uh-huh."

"Deidre, sweetheart, would you tell me if you thought I was being a bad, unnatural mother? I mean, if you're thinking that and not saying it, I'll kill you."

Deidre laughed and then felt angry. She hated this trick of her mother's, saying something funny at a dramatic moment. It made everything seem trivial. "No, it's not . . . it's not about morality. I mean, I don't believe people should just fool around, but you guys are old enough . . . I mean, if you feel that way, I don't see why you shouldn't . . . but—I don't know, if I act funny when you tell me these things, it's because this is all new to me too. I'm just not used to stuff like that happening to you. So every time there's a new thing . . ."

"I know."

"But, jeez, Mom, if it's like you said . . . if you really have been going around depressed all these years, you'd better not blow this thing, you know."

"I didn't mean I was depressed every minute. I just meant—"

"I know. But . . . look, would you do two things for me?"

"What?"

"Well, bring me a T-shirt from Sarasota and . . ." Deidre lowered her eyes suddenly.

Her mother squeezed her shoulder. "What, baby?"

Deidre looked up. Her voice came out strangled. "Would *you* cook dinner for *me* tonight?"

Mrs. Holland looked completely astonished. "But I can't cook! You know that! My dinners are *horrible.*"

Deidre brushed the back of her hand across her eyes. "Every once in a while you get sick of good food," she explained.

I

Curt rolled over, partially on top of Susie, and kissed her. Deidre tried not to think about his bare torso, first against the prickly shag carpet, then grazing the exposed flesh between the top and bottom of Susie's swimsuit. She should never have agreed to hang out with them today. They were like two puppies in heat, always doing things that made Deidre want to stare and look away at the same time. But she missed Susie. She hadn't seen her in over a week and the only way to see Susie these days was to see Curt. Besides, Jeff was obsessed with finishing his composition and hadn't come to the pool for three days in a row.

So, she'd agreed to go swimming at Curt's pool. It was bad enough when they were in the water, watching

Susie and Curt grope each other and threaten to pull each other's pants down, but here, back at his apartment, they had stopped looking playful. Deidre couldn't believe they could carry on like that in front of a witness. She would never do that and she felt Jeff wouldn't either.

Susie was sort of pretending not to notice Curt. She had been lying supine on the rug with one arm over her eyes. Curt had been stretched out next to her, on his stomach, watching a Reds game on TV. His family was originally from Cincinnati. Deidre sat behind both of them, curled up on the couch. She had changed back into her clothes and dried her hair but the young lovers hadn't bothered or didn't want to. They preferred to drip dry, using their own body heat for evaporation.

Deidre had spent the past half hour struggling to concentrate on the ball game, but really staring at the seat of Curt's trunks. It was impossible to do otherwise. His body was different from Jeff's, which she'd also had the opportunity to scrutinize in swimwear. Jeff was a big rack, with broad shoulders and strong legs, but narrow hips and flat, little-boy buttocks. But Curt was almost the opposite. He was sinewy, with a long, catlike shape to his shoulders and back, which drew the eye inevitably to his backside, where the graceful line swelled into two perfect curves of black spandex. His trunks weren't brief, but they were cut to hug the body and cup in at the thighs. They were old too. The material was worn and nubby and there was a lighter spot where the fabric was wearing through.

Deidre squirmed and shifted her position. She knew she should get out of there. She was getting a very uncomfortable feeling in a very uncomfortable place.

Curt's first kiss had failed to "awaken" Susie, and he was responding to the challenge now, kissing her more passionately and bumping his body against hers. The black spandex pitched and rolled.

Deidre's physical discomfort became sharp and intense. She didn't know if she could get up and leave even if she wanted to.

Luckily, Sleeping Beauty suddenly pushed him off. "Cut it out!" she said.

He rolled away, looking dazed. Deidre could now see the *front* of his swimsuit, where his emotions were apparent. "Bitch!" he said to Susie. "Whirlpool! Amana! Westinghouse!"

Susie sat up and yawned. "If I'm a refrigerator, you're an oven," she told him. "And your thermostat is stuck."

"Be careful," he said, reaching out with mock menace. "I might burn you."

Susie ducked his embrace and stood up, flipping her wet hair back. "I'm going to get dressed," she said.

He watched her walk down the hall, then turned to Deidre. "She's really crazy about me." He sighed. "But she tries to cover it up with this really good act that I make her sick."

Now that he was sitting on the most provocative part

of his anatomy, Deidre's physical discomfort was receding to a dull, unpleasant throb. It was like having a foot go to sleep, she thought. Coming out of it felt worse than when it was happening. "I wish you guys wouldn't do that in front of me," she said. "It makes me . . . uncomfortable."

His sassafras eyes gazed at her innocently. "I'm sorry!" he said. "I didn't even think about it. All I was thinking about was your friend and her little rainbow bikini. Would you please tell me something?"

Almost normal now. She stretched her legs out in front of her. Her spine, which had been rigid, relaxed. "What?"

"If she hates having me all over her, how come she wears that little suit made out of shoestrings? Doesn't she know what that does to a guy? I mean, she could wear a normal swimsuit like yours. She bought that for some reason, didn't she?"

"She probably bought it because she likes it," Deidre said. "How come guys always think women do everything for them? Do you think women think about men all the time?"

He blinked. "Sure! I think about women all the time."

"Anyway, you don't always know what will turn somebody else on." Little did he know what his ratty old trunks did for her! "Maybe Susie doesn't realize the effect her clothes have on you."

"Bullshit, bullshit, bullshit," he said. "But enough

171

about her. How's your love life? How's the piano player?"

"Okay," Deidre said. Then something strange came over her. Maybe it was the thrill of having this handsome older guy talk to her. Maybe it was jealousy over Susie's luck. But something made Deidre sit up and assume an expression of studied casualness, the look adults take on when they brag. "I've been to the club by myself a few times, since we went."

"Yeah?" he said. "How do you get over there without a car?"

She shrugged. "Take the bus. Jeff usually drives me home. I could probably drive in with him if I wanted to, but I like to just show up at the club and surprise him."

"Yeah? You guys are getting to be pretty close, aren't you?"

Deidre inspected her fingernails. "I guess so. He really needs someone to talk to. He just got out of a pretty bad relationship and, of course, his career puts him under a lot of pressure."

"You're kidding. What pressure? I'd love his job. Just sit in a bar all night and get free drinks and have women fall all over you. . . ."

"He's not that kind of person!" Deidre said. "You don't understand. He's a serious musician. Working in that bar is killing him, grinding his spirit down to nothing. He belongs in a symphony orchestra or some kind of really elegant club at the very least. You can't even imagine the kind of courage it takes to strive for things you might not ever get and to—" She suddenly realized she was babbling and Curt was staring at her, wide eyed.

"I'm sorry," he said. "I didn't know."

"I know," she said. "I'm sorry."

"You're really close to the guy."

"Well, I'm someone he can talk to. Like, the other night. Thank goodness I was at the club. It was one of those times when the pressure got too high and he started drinking and messing up his show—it was horrible."

Curt was mesmerized. "What happened?"

Deidre felt elated and scared, as if she were walking a tightrope. "Oh, I straightened him out. I took his keys and called us a cab and I took him home and made him some coffee and we talked." Her heart was pounding. "And we kissed."

"Wow."

"He's working on a piece of music he wants to name after me."

"Wow. Your mother know you do all this?"

"No. She wouldn't understand. She's . . . out a lot at night."

"Oh. Like mother, like daughter, huh? Boy. Still waters run deep. Isn't this guy worried about your age? Does he know fourteen'll get him twenty?"

She looked at him scornfully. "Jeff doesn't care about age. He probably thinks I'm a lot older. He's never asked."

"Hmmm." He scooted closer to her. When the light from the window caught the spandex just right, it made it glisten. "Tell me. Do you and he—"

"Here I am! Hold the applause!" Susie emerged from the back hall, dressed and fluffy, carrying a pair of Curt's jeans. "Here!" she said. "Cover yourself. What are you two guys doing all huddled up like that?" Her tone was playful but her eyes looked a little dangerous.

"Deidre's telling me about her love life," Curt said. "With the piano man. Hot stuff." He stood up and stepped into his jeans. "Anybody want a beer?"

"No," said Deidre.

"Yes," said Susie.

"You shouldn't do that," Deidre told her.

"You're not my mother!"

"Two beers and a Coke for Mother!" Curt said. He loped away, pulling up his zipper.

"What were you telling him?" Susie asked.

"Something that happened a couple of nights ago. I went to the club and Jeff was upset and he had too much to drink."

"Oh, wow!"

"No! No! No! I called him a cab and helped him up to his apartment."

"And put him to bed?" Susie flashed a dimple.

"No! God. All you think about . . . what happened was really nice and sweet and romantic, if *you* can imagine that. I made him some coffee and we talked and he really opened up to me . . . and at the end of the evening I kissed him."

"You kissed him?"

"Yes."

"I can't believe it. Did he like it?"

Deidre smiled modestly. "He acted like he did. He's having a midlife crisis. Do you know how old he is? Twenty-six!"

"Oh, God!"

"So naturally, he's depressed. His birthday is next Friday and I don't know what to do. I want to do something special to cheer him up."

Curt came back with the refreshments and passed them out.

"Bake a cake," Susie said. "That's your thing."

"More than that," Deidre said. "It has to be something really special."

Curt popped his top. "What'd I miss?"

Deidre opened her Coke and waited patiently for the fizz to die down. "Jeff's birthday is Friday and I want to do something special for him."

Curt laughed wickedly.

"Shut up!" Susie said. "This is serious. Deidre said Jeff is feeling down—"

"And you want to get him up?" Curt said.

Susie slapped his shoulder. "I *told* you—"

Curt suddenly jumped to his feet, sloshing beer on the carpet. "And I told you I don't like to be knocked around like that!" he shouted. "Cut it out!"

"I'm sorry," she said, cringing. "I was just playing! I didn't hurt you, for God's sake."

"Well . . . I don't like it!" he repeated. He ran his hand up through his hair, looking embarrassed. "Okay?"

"Okay!" Susie said.

He sat down, flushed. "I'm sorry, Deidre. What did you say?"

Deidre was a little shaken, but she decided the best policy would be to divert him. "Jeff is depressed because he's getting older now and he's not happy with his life and I have to do something special for him, so he won't drink and brood all night."

"She doesn't think a cake is enough," Susie added.

"Bake a cake and jump out of it," Curt said. He slid out of Susie's slapping range, giggling.

"Come on, be serious!" Susie said. "Why don't you give him a surprise party? Do you know any of his friends?"

Deidre stiffened. "His friends are all bimbos from the bar!"

"Oh, boy!" said Curt. "Can I come?"

Susie forgot or acted on reflex and slapped his face.

The next moment was a blur. Curt flew at Susie, grabbing her shoulders and slamming her on her back. At the same time he said, in what could only be called a growl, "I . . . told . . . you . . . not . . . to . . . DO . . . THAT!" His fingers were digging into her arms and he was panting. His eyes were terrifying.

176

Deidre was frozen in place. Susie began to cry.

Then the spell that held Curt seemed to break. One by one his bunched-up muscles let go, his grip loosened, his eyes softened. Still panting heavily, he let Susie go and stood up, backing away. He looked at his hands as if he didn't know what they might do next.

Susie rolled over into a kind of fetal position and sobbed freely. Deidre felt dizzy and realized she'd been holding her breath. She let it out slowly.

Curt had a look of fear in his eyes. He put his hand up to his mouth as if he were going to be sick. "Oh, God!" he wailed. "I'm sorry!"

Susie's response was to sob harder, covering her face with her hands.

Curt said wildly, "I didn't mean to!"

Susie was recovering now and wanted revenge. "You bastard!" she sobbed out, looking at him blindly through her tears. "I never want to see you again!"

"Okay," he said softly. He looked ready to cry himself.

"Let's get out of here!" Susie said, trying to stand up on shaky legs. Deidre still couldn't move.

Curt sank into a chair, hugging and rocking himself. "I'm sorry, Susie," he said softly. "I didn't mean to. I really didn't mean to."

"Come on!" Susie said to Deidre.

"Wait a minute," Deidre said, watching him.

"Come on!" Susie screamed.

"Go ahead and go," Curt said, looking defeated.

"Don't worry!" Susie said. "I don't put up with shit like that. What makes you think you can treat people that way?"

Curt looked up. "I'm crazy!" he said. "Feel better? All this time you've been messing around with a lunatic!"

Susie was calm now but still angry. "Well, *I'm* not crazy," she said. "And if there's one thing I know enough not to do, it's to get mixed up with a guy who would—"

"Can I just explain one thing?"

"No way!"

Tears came into his eyes. "Susan, please."

Deidre didn't want to hear his explanation at all. She just wanted to get out of there in one piece. But Susie had sat back down on the carpet and was rummaging roughly in her purse for Kleenex. "You've got one minute."

Curt had stopped rocking but he still hugged himself. "Sometimes I can't control my temper," he said. "It's inherited. My father is a . . . violent person."

Susie blew her nose. "What do you mean?"

He lowered his eyes. "He beats me up."

"Like . . . all the time?"

"Yeah."

Susie blushed. "What exactly does he do? I mean is it like . . . spanking?"

He shook his head. "Slugging. Punching. Kicking. I've been to the hospital once or twice."

"Oh, God!"

He raised his eyes sadly. "So, it's in the blood, I guess. I can't help it. I'm really sorry, though. But if you don't want to go out anymore I don't blame you. I never wanted you to see this side of me. I thought with you I could start over. Everybody at school knows about me. I've been getting in fights since I was a kid. I was scared to death you'd mention my name to your sister and she'd tell you how screwed up I am."

Susie looked sympathetic now. "Can't you get counseling or something?"

"I've had it off and on. It doesn't help. I was born with this. My old man can't help it either. He's always as sorry as hell when we're cleaning up the blood."

Deidre finally found her voice. "I don't think it's inherited, Curt. I think it's more like something you react to. I mean, you were okay until Susie started hitting you. That must set you off because . . . you know."

"Yeah, maybe."

Susie was twisting a Kleenex in her hand. "Maybe I could try real hard not to hit you or set you off," she said.

He looked up. "Really?"

She shrugged. "It could be like probation. I'll be careful and we'll see. But if you ever do anything scary like that again . . ."

"I won't! I swear! God! Nobody's ever given me a second chance before. I swear, I'll try so hard . . ."

"Okay," Susie said softly.

He got up slowly, walked over to Susie, and knelt in

front of her. She pulled him into her arms. His body jerked violently. Deidre realized he was crying and thoughtfully went to the bathroom, even though she didn't have to.

I

They wound up the day at the mall eating ice cream. Somehow the events of the day had drawn all three closer. Trying to stay on light topics, they discussed Jeff's birthday surprise again.

"I have the key to his apartment," Deidre said. "I was thinking of letting myself in and cooking dinner for him when he comes home from work. He's always complaining he never gets a decent dinner."

"And you're such a good cook," Susie said. "But doesn't he get home from work pretty late?"

Deidre shrugged. "Midnight. One at the latest. So I'll call it supper." She knew this reference was over their heads, but sometimes she liked to flaunt her knowledge of the History of Civilized Dining.

"What about your mom?" Susie asked. "You're going to leave the house at midnight and tell her you're cooking dinner for a twenty-six-year-old man?"

"No! Mom's going away for the weekend. I can do whatever I want."

"She is? Is she doing something with that orchid man?"

Deidre nodded, coloring up a little.

"Oh, wow! You didn't tell me they were—"

"It's pretty serious," Deidre said. "Don't tell Aunt Carol."

"I wouldn't. God. How do you feel about all this?"

Deidre blushed. "Well . . . I really wouldn't mind if they got married, you know? He's kind of nice. But right now, when they have to sneak around and act guilty, I don't like that too much. My mom acts so . . . I don't know. It irritates me."

"Wish my dad would get a woman," Curt said. "I'd love to have him go away some weekend."

Both girls looked at him anxiously.

"Lighten up!" he snapped. "This isn't *Donahue*!" Then to make up for that, he said, "I think that's a nice idea, Deidre. About cooking. Guys love that. I mean, I'd be knocked out by something like that."

"What if things get . . . too romantic?" Susie asked.

"Jeff's not like that," Deidre said. "I mean, I wish he'd be a little *more* aggressive. I think he's confused about our ages. He doesn't want to scare me off. But if I could get the mood right . . . I know he's lonely. It could get interesting." Her heart beat fast. She could picture every moment of it.

"You wouldn't stay up there all night, would you?" Susie asked. She stirred her ice cream into soup.

"No. We'd eat and talk and maybe fool around just a little. I'd leave about two or three, I guess. Or I'd stay on his couch all night. Whichever."

Susie looked at Curt. "Are you thinking what I'm thinking?"

"Maybe," he said softly.

Susie looked at Deidre. "Could Curt and I spend the night in your apartment?"

Deidre sat up. "What do you mean?"

Susie lifted a spoonful of melted ice cream and let it drizzle back into the dish. "Curt and I . . . one time we talked about . . . how nice it would be to sleep together."

"You guys!" Deidre said.

"No!" Susie said. "I mean really *sleep*. You know. Cuddle up like married people and wake up together. . . ."

"Don't put her on the spot," Curt muttered. He looked embarrassed.

"I guess you could," Deidre said. "If you promise not to drink or mess up the house. Just use my room, not Mom's. And when I come home, I'll just lie down on the couch. If I come home." The idea of cuddling up like married people sounded appealing.

"You really wouldn't mind?" Curt asked.

"No, it's okay." Deidre turned to Susie. "What will you tell Aunt Carol?"

Susie laughed. "I'll tell her I'm staying over at your place!" she said. "That's the truth!"

"Nobody cares if I'm out all night!" Curt said cheerfully.

Susie looked at Curt. "Do you promise to be good?"

He held up his hand. "On my honor as a Scout."

Susie put a straw in her melted ice cream and slurped. "Boy! This is going to be exciting!"

Deidre agreed. She was so excited, it felt almost like a heart attack.

·13·

It was raining in Paris. The sky was heavy with clouds. Drops of water collected in the petals of the wisteria. The Eiffel Tower was a black silhouette against the sky. Deidre's table had an umbrella, however, so she didn't mind. Jeff was late, as usual. He was always losing his watch, or forgetting to put it on. Deidre had gotten used to it over the years, and had learned to order a little snack while she waited. Today she was drinking hot tea with lemon and eating pâté and water biscuits. She looked at her watch. Three-thirty. He was supposed to meet her at two. This was bad even for him. She had hoped to go to a few galleries before dinner. She began to fidget, from a combination of anger and worry.

The waiter checked on her. She waved him away. She was just about to get up and leave when she saw him across the street, cutting through the park with his heavy, clumsy jog, raincoat flapping like wings. Deidre smiled to herself, signaled the waiter, and ordered him a rum and tonic. Then she folded her arms and settled back in her chair, watching his halting progress across the boulevard, brakes screeching and horns honking in his wake. He loped up to the table and flopped into his chair.

"I'm really late," he scolded himself, smiling coyly to see if he was forgiven.

She kept her arms folded. "Where were you?" she asked, playfully stern.

He shrugged. "Shopping. And I got lost once. Well, really, twice."

"Did you eat lunch?" she asked as the waiter set his drink in front of him.

"What's this?" he said, pleased. "Lunch? No, I guess I didn't. I was shopping up a storm."

"Another order of pâté," Deidre said to the waiter. "What did you buy?"

"Hmmm?" He tasted his drink.

"You did so much shopping. What did you buy?"

"I'll show you in a minute. What did you do all day?"

"I was shopping too. I bought a ewer and some sauté pans."

He frowned. "Well, I know what a sauté pan is. . . ."

"A ewer is a little pitcher for oil."

"Oh, right!" he said. "Now you did it. That's what I was going to get you for Christmas."

"Very funny. What did you buy?"

He looked at her with wide, innocent eyes. "You want to see it right now?"

185

"Yes!"

"Oh, okay." He dug in his raincoat pocket and fished out a little jeweler's box, holding it out to Deidre.

Deidre looked at the box, then at him. "Did you buy yourself some cuff links?"

He laughed. "Look and see."

She opened the box. It was a diamond solitaire, gleaming dully in the rainy light. "Jeff . . ."

"I don't know if it will look good on me, though," he said. "Do you want to wear it?"

"Oh, Jeff," Deidre said, fighting tears. "I didn't expect this here . . . now. . . ."

He smiled. "I figured this trip would make you vulnerable. I'm a crafty devil."

"Yes, you are." She took the ring and slid it on her finger.

"Don't do that unless you mean business!" he said. "Once it's on, if you back out, I'll sue you for breach of promise!"

"Don't worry." She looked at the soft, smoky rainbows in the ring, and then up at the sky and all around, memorizing the details of this moment: the leaden clouds, the reflections of traffic lights in the wet pavement, the wisteria, and Jeff—hair tousled, raincoat flapping, gazing at her as if nothing else in the world mattered.

∎

It could happen, Deidre thought. *It could happen just like that.* If she was careful, if she coaxed it along, just right. If she never tried to get too much, too soon. The age difference was a big problem now, but it would lessen with time. She knew, as surely as she had ever known anything, she was the right person for him. That whole incident at the bar had proved it. He was just a big, scared, lost child who needed looking after. She had handled the situation so capably, taking his keys, seeing him home, making coffee, helping him talk it out. She knew instinctively, Chrissie would not have nurtured him that way. She would have berated him and made him feel worthless. That was why that relationship had ended.

And now his life was at a crossroads. He was composing that rhapsody to find himself. It was no accident he had chosen her name for the title. He wanted someone to believe in him. Someone who would watch his drinking and make him eat regular meals and tell him he was her hero. Everything in Deidre's temperament suited her for the role, and Jeff knew it too. That was why, almost without realizing it, he had been reaching out to her all summer.

Tonight would be a crucial step forward. It was his birthday and he would be all alone. He would come home depressed, probably drunk, thinking no one cared about him.

And there it would all be. His table set with good china and silver. Candles. A vase of carnations. Smoked salmon. A strawberry-endive salad with raspberry vin-aigrette. Veal roasted and stuffed with rosemary. Artichokes and mushrooms in lemon-butter. Oven-fried potatoes. A perfect merlot. Peach cream pie. Coffee. A beautifully wrapped, well-chosen gift lying at his place setting. And Deidre herself in her favorite dress: a deep hyacinth-blue with lace at the wrists and throat, a ribbon to match threaded in her hair. He would talk and she would listen. He would hurt and she would care. Somewhere in the back of his mind it would dawn on him that he needed her, that she was the answer to all his prayers.

She didn't want to think past that. He might want to tell her his feelings. He might try to kiss her. Maybe like Curt, his passion would carry him away and he would try something else. She wasn't afraid. She knew she could handle him, slow him down, remind him that this was serious. They needed to take their time. Maybe they would sit up the rest of the night, talking and making plans. She pictured them on his couch together, watching the sun come up. She was leaning back against his shoulder. He was playing sleepily with the ribbons in her hair.

"Cyril! Get down!" Deidre cried. He was standing in Jeff's place setting, lapping up water from the flower vase. He looked at her blandly, his expression saying, clearly, *You aren't my mother!*

"Get down!" she screamed, flapping a dish towel at him.

He jumped to the floor and hissed at her before taking refuge behind the rocking horse. Deidre took the plate to the sink and squirted soap on it, fighting back tears. She was upset all out of proportion. Her hands were trembling. It was just the idea of anything going wrong. She felt the evening had to proceed flawlessly from beginning to end or it would all unravel somehow. Of course that was silly. She dried and polished the plate and freshened the flowers, forcing herself to breathe calmly and slowly. Then she went to the rocking horse to apologize.

"I'm sorry, kitty," she said to the quivering ball of outraged fur.

Cyril flattened his ears and bugged out his eyes like a Chinese demon. Deidre considered shutting him in the bedroom. He had been angry with her all evening.

She'd done most of the cooking downstairs, of course, in her own apartment. She'd started early this morning, peeling, pitting, and pureeing peaches for the pie, mixing the vinaigrette, preparing and stuffing the veal, carefully wrapping the gift. Then, when she was sure Jeff had left for work, she'd packed everything into a huge hamper and brought it all up to finish. Cyril had been furious at her using a key to let herself in and had sulked in the corners of the room, planning sabotage. He had jumped on the stove when she started the vegetables. He'd tried to chew the ribbon on Jeff's package. And now this.

Still, she was reluctant to pen him up. Jeff was crazy

about him and might be angry. Anyway, the damn litter box was in the hall. If she put the cat in the bedroom
and he had an accident . . . well, that would not con-
tribute to a romantic atmosphere. She decided to try
and make peace. She went and got a turkey frank from
the refrigerator. "Hey, big fella . . ." She squatted
down and held it out to him. "Don't you want to be
friends? I might be your mommy, someday."

Cyril snatched the hot dog and bolted for the bedroom.

"And if I am, I'll send you away to boarding school!"
she called after him.

It was close to midnight. Time to take stock. She
expected Jeff between twelve-thirty and one. Still,
she'd have no serious problems if he was late. Like all
good chefs Deidre knew how to hold and rewarm food
without ruining it. Right now there was nothing left to
do. The roast and the potatoes were finishing up in the
oven, looking brown and beautiful. The vegetables
were covered on the stove, waiting for a quick reheat.
There was a basket of homemade bread on the table
and a cut-glass dish of honey. The salad and pie were
chilling. The wine was open and breathing. When he
came, she would light the candles.

With everything so well in hand Deidre knew what
was going to happen now. She had been busy cooking
since she came in but now there was time for a quick,
furtive snoop. She had been tempted by his desk the
other time, so she went there now and pulled out the

lap drawer quietly, like someone afraid of tripping an alarm.

There was a wonderful array of junk inside; a perfect portrait of Jeff's personality. Felt-tip markers in candy colors, safety scissors of the kind little children use, legal pads covered with mysterious financial calculations and doodles of cats and bears, a box of adhesive gold stars, a ruler from the Flowers Bread Factory, a glow-in-the-dark yo-yo, a pair of glasses with a false nose and mustache, a faded, ripped Yankees cap, a stash of Bit-O-Honeys, a key chain with a blue fried marble, the sheet music to Gershwin's Concerto in F, match folders, corks, swizzle sticks, the blue exercise book in which he was writing *Deidre.* Seeing her name in his handwriting on the cover made her shiver. There was a stack of birthday cards he'd just received; from his parents, from his sister, Beth, from "Aunt Betty and Uncle Dale," from Nicki the bartender, from someone named Steve and someone who called himself "The Phantom." All were humorous cards, playfully insulting. *No one takes him seriously but me,* Deidre thought. *I'm the only one who understands how much pain this birthday is causing him.*

Then she found the letter. Even before she knew what it was she recoiled involuntarily, as if her fingers had touched something hot. She felt dazed, like a sleepwalker, as she slowly took it out and put it on the desktop.

It was a plain white envelope, not colored or scented

as she would have expected. It was hand addressed to Jeff with a preprinted return label—*Christine Wilson, 62 Monet Court, Tamarac.* Deidre read it over and over, memorizing. Not because it was *her* address, but because it had once been Jeff's.

It was jaggedly torn open. He had done it angrily with his finger. And right after he read it, he'd put it back in the envelope and shut it in the drawer. What did that mean? It meant he was thinking about it. He didn't know what to make of it. He'd put it on hold. The postmark was three days ago. Deidre took the letter out and unfolded it. It was handwritten, black ink on plain white paper. A strong, slanting, impatient hand.

> **Happy birthday, you creep.**
>
> **Since you won't talk to me on the phone I guess I have to write you, even though I'm not good at this and I have no idea what I want to say.**
>
> **That's a lie. I know what I want to say but I don't have the guts to say it. I miss you. I really, really miss you. I didn't think I would at first. When you moved out, I thought, good. Recess is over. Now I can live like a grown-up. Get back to reality.**
>
> **But reality sucks, dear. Maybe you've done something to me, wrecked me for a normal relationship. I've dated a few guys, just the kind I thought I wanted and they were sad, pathetic evenings, let me tell you. I know you've done a little better. I called**

once when she was there and, like a silly kid, I hung up. She's probably more mature than me and never screams at you or makes your life a living hell, like I did.

So why am I writing? I can't help it. It's going to be your birthday and I'm going to sit around and remember last year when we went to the Keys and I had, probably, the best time of my life. I guess I just want you to know I'm suffering, because I know I made you suffer and it's only fair I let you have your revenge.

And in case you ever get bored with all your happiness and freedom and you want somebody to yell at you and treat you like a child, I'm still around and I still love you.

Chrissie

P.S. I miss your big, sloppy, bad-tempered cat too.

Deidre folded the letter back up and shoved it roughly into the envelope and slammed the drawer. The last thing she wanted was to feel sympathy for that bitch.

"You had your chance!" she said to the drawer. "You had your chance and you blew it!"

She stood up and walked around the room, thinking. It was good she had found the letter. It was important to understand what she was up against. This evening was more crucial than she had thought. He might be wavering. He needed to know, right now, there was a better alternative. There was someone who would never scream at him. There was someone who could encourage and inspire him and fill his life with flowers and music and good meals and give him the environment he needed to do his work. He hadn't composed anything when he was with *her*, had he? No! He'd been too busy fighting and defending himself. It was Deidre who could bring out the best in him and tonight she would show him that.

The latch clicked. Deidre nearly screamed. She quickly smoothed her hair and her dress and lit the candles. Her heart beat like a jackhammer. She had the strange, irrational fear that somehow all this might make him angry, make him hate her forever.

He trudged in with the weary look of all workers coming home after a long shift. His sport coat was over his shoulder and his hair was mussed by the wind. Then he looked with confusion toward the candlelight. He came to a complete stop, looking at Deidre, the table, the kitchen. From that moment on all his movements had the jerky, halting quality animals assume in a strange environment. "What is this?" he said quietly.

She took a few steps forward. "Happy birthday."

He frowned. "Oh," he said. There was a moment of silence. He walked slowly into the dining area and circled the table, looking at the china, the crystal, the candles, the flowers. He picked up his package and put it down. All this time he was frowning.

Nervous, Deidre began to babble. "I wanted to do something special for you. I know . . . I mean, I think I understand this birthday is hard for you. I wanted to do something to let you know—"

"How did you get in here?" he interrupted. "Does your mother know you're here? It's almost one in the morning!"

He almost *did* seem angry. "She's gone for the whole weekend. So it's okay. You don't have to worry. And I used the key under the mat, because . . . I wanted to surprise you."

He was in the kitchen now, prowling around the stove. "You went to so much *trouble*," he accused.

"I wanted to! I told you! Anyway, cooking is what I like to do, remember? And you told me once you hated coming home night after night and eating garbage. Remember? You said it had been so long since you had a nice dinner?"

"Yeah . . ." There was something grudging in his voice, as if he wanted Deidre to convince him of something before he would relax.

Deidre's fingers were wrestling each other. "Are you angry with me?" she blurted out. She felt a lump in her throat. This wasn't the way she'd pictured it at all. He was supposed to be awed, joyful, not . . . suspicious. *That* was how he looked! As if he thought she was trying to pull something!

"Angry?" he asked himself. "No, I'm not angry. But

this is so . . ." He gestured toward the table. "I didn't expect it, that's all."

"I thought you said you liked surprises."

"I thought I did too."

Deidre was near tears. "Do you want me to leave?"

He looked at her closely. His face softened. "No. No, sweetheart. I'm sorry. I'm acting like a jerk here, I guess. I just didn't realize . . . you're such a nice person. You do all these things for me. You're always surprising me that way. Nobody's ever . . . fussed over me like this before. I guess I don't know how to take it. I certainly didn't mean to act like I don't appreciate it. God. This is all just . . . *beautiful*."

Deidre let out a long breath. "Open your present," she said. "While I get the food ready."

She listened to him ripping the paper off as she took the roast and potatoes from the oven. They were perfect. She basted the meat lovingly and turned on a flame under the vegetables.

"Oh, wow!" he called.

She went to the kitchen doorway. He was sitting at his place, flipping eagerly through the *Songwriter's Market*. "It's got everything you need to know," she explained. "How to publish your music, places to send it to get it played, what to do about agents and legal advisors, everything."

"I see," he said happily. "This is exactly what I need!" He looked up at her. "You can't wait to make your name a household word, is that it?" he teased.

"I don't care about that. But it's a beautiful piece of music and it deserves to be heard."

Now he looked the way she'd imagined. His eyes were shining with warmth. He held out his arms. "Come here, you," he said.

Trembling, she came forward. Because he was sitting and she was standing, he put his arms around her waist and rested his cheek against her stomach. She put a tentative arm around his shoulders, looking down on the crown of blond hair, feeling dizzy, wondering if she could dare to give him a little kiss on top of the head. She rested her cheek there instead. Her whole body flooded with waves of comfort and warmth, the kind she hadn't felt since she was a little girl, snuggling under the covers, listening to bedtime stories. He was murmuring things, too, telling her his feelings. "You don't know what you've done for me," he was saying softly. "You came along at a time when I felt like absolute hell and you've been so kind and sweet. You'll never know what a difference you've made."

That was the way he talked in her fantasies! It was coming true! It was all coming true!

He let go of her then and sat up, reaching for the book to cover his embarrassment. "I won't let you down, kid," he said. "I'll study this thing and we'll get your rhapsody into every symphony hall in the country. Okay?"

"Okay," she said, not sure if she was laughing or crying, but just knowing she was happy. "Let me get your dinner."

The next hour and a half were magical. They sat across the candlelit table like lovers in a restaurant. All of the food turned out perfectly. Jeff sipped wine and Deidre drank bottled water from a champagne glass. They talked about silly, irrelevant things in their childhoods—good and bad birthday parties, camping trips, recurring nightmares. Jeff told how his father went through elaborate rituals to chase "monsters" out of the closets and Deidre felt, for the first time, there was something she'd missed out on.

By the time they finished the pie it was two-thirty. Deidre cleared the table and served coffee in the living room. Cyril, who'd been sulking in the bedroom all evening, finally slunk out and took up his position on the piano. Deidre felt it was a good omen.

"I'll never forget this as long as I live," Jeff told her. "I thought this was going to be a horrible night and you made it really wonderful."

"My pleasure." Deidre clinked her cup against his.

"You must be tired," he said. "You did all that work and it's really late."

"I *told* you," she said. "Cooking is not work to me. And I'm not tired at all."

He put his hand on her shoulder. "It's pretty late for a little girl like you to be up."

Deidre put her fingers over his fingers. "I'm not such a little girl," she said softly.

They held each other's eyes. "Yes, you are," he said faintly.

Deidre moved a little closer to him. "You want me to show you?" she asked. She put her hands on his shoulders and slowly leaned in toward him, smelling his cologne, feeling the heat of him, lifting her chin and brushing her lips gently against his. Just the way she'd done before. . . .

"Hey!" he shouted, ducking, pulling away. "God *damn* you! What are you trying to do!"

Deidre was not used to being shouted at. Tears welled up. "I thought . . ." she began.

He had jumped up and was pacing. "You thought what? Is that what all this was about? That's what I thought when I first came in, but I thought, no, she's too nice for that! This is just great! You did all that crap just to soften me up so I'd teach you some tricks! Is that the idea?"

His anger and his whole speech confused Deidre. The room was a blur from tears. "No!" she choked out. "No!"

"I guess this would be a fun game for somebody your age!" he raved on. "See if you can get the lonely guy worked up! That it? I mean, you know how pathetic I am. I guess you figured me for easy prey. Then you could tell all the kids in school about it later, huh? You can say, 'For a second there, I really had the poor bastard *going*. . . .'"

"No!" she sobbed out, clenching her fists. "No, you're wrong!"

"What have I got wrong?" he demanded, shouting right in her face. "Jeez! I thought you *liked* me. I guess all those nice things you did were just part of this . . . campaign. So if I fell for it, how far were you going to let me go before you cut me off? How much of a fool were you going to let me be?"

"You don't understand!" Deidre screamed. She was in some kind of rage, but still crying. "I *love* you!"

"Oh, shit!" he shouted. He walked away from her and sat down with his back to her. "Sure," he added.

Deidre couldn't control herself at all. She pulled her knees up to her chest and sobbed. She had nothing. She had put all her love, all her energy, all her hope into . . . nothing! She didn't know or understand this man at all. He didn't even care that she was crying. He just sat there with his back to her, indifferent. The momentum of her crying gradually slowed down, but the rage was still building and feeding on itself. She looked at the floor, where he'd thrown the wrapping from his present. It was all in shreds. He'd torn into it like an animal. She'd taken forever to wrap that package and he'd clawed right into it. When Deidre opened a package, she slid her thumbnail under the tape at just one end and carefully slid the box out, leaving the wrapping whole. The prettiest ones she saved in a drawer. She had *respect* for things! "I *hate* you!" she screamed at his back.

"You just said you loved me," he muttered, not looking around. "You better make up your mind."

Something in his tone put her over the edge. He seemed to be taking all this as some kind of joke. It was the end of her world, and he regarded it as just another messed-up evening. She suddenly jumped up and ran at him, pummeling his back and shoulders with her fists, kicking at him.

"Hey!" he shouted. He whirled around and grabbed her wrists. "Hey!"

They were struggling like that when they heard the screams from downstairs. It was a female scream at first, some kind of shouting, like a domestic tirade, but that was interrupted by the male voice, and his scream was not the ordinary shouting of an argument. It was a high-pitched, animallike roar. It came once and then again and again. Both Jeff and Deidre had frozen in their positions to listen to the strangeness of it. Then it stopped and there was complete silence.

Jeff let go of Deidre because she had stopped fighting him. "Oh, my God," she said, as she turned and ran for the door. *"Susie!"*

·14·

Deidre took the stairs at a gallop, not wanting to wait for the elevator. Her apartment was ominously silent as she frantically twisted the key in the lock, too panicky to make it work. "Come *on*!" she wailed at the lock, the key, the universe. Sweat broke out on her face. Her legs were shaking. She heard heavy footsteps coming up behind her.

"Here." Jeff took the key from her hand and fitted it neatly in the lock. The door swung open.

Susie was near the door, standing with her knees bent as if she would be ready at any moment to drop into a crouch. Tears ran down her face and she was naked to the waist, holding her arms across her breasts. Her terrified gaze went across the room to Curt, who was huddled in a corner, knees clasped to his chest, motionless and staring, as if in a trance. His shirt was also missing.

Across the room, near the couch, there was broken glass and spilled beer cans and an amber stain on the wall, with little rivulets still trickling down from it. Two T-shirts and a bra rested among the couch cushions.

Deidre was too frightened and confused to take it all in, but Jeff came past her into the room. He unbuttoned and removed his shirt and handed it to Susie without looking at her. Then he walked slowly toward Curt, making some kind of calculation. "Are these friends of yours?" he asked Deidre. "Did you know they were here?"

"Yes. It's my cousin and her boyfriend."

He turned to Susie, who was still fumbling with his shirt buttons. "What happened?"

"He . . ." Susie said. She was shaking so badly, she could hardly do the buttons and she began to cry in frustration. She turned to Deidre. "I *know* we promised not to drink. . . ." She sobbed. "But he just wanted to bring up a six-pack."

Deidre couldn't take her eyes off Curt. There was something terrifying about him. He didn't seem to be listening to or following anything that was going on. He was just breathing out and breathing in, looking at something in the middle distance, like someone watching an invisible TV screen.

"What's his name?" Jeff asked.

"Curt," Susie whispered.

"Curt?" Jeff called. "You hear me, buddy?"

Deidre felt cold all over. At the sound of his name Curt didn't look up, but his lips curved into a faintly sinister smile, as if someone in the room had made a distasteful joke.

"He's not completely out of it," Jeff said. "I think that's good. I saw this once before. It happened to somebody in my dorm in college. It looks a lot worse than it is. I mean, he's bad off now, but I think they're supposed to come out of it." He turned back to Susie. "You answer me," he commanded. "What happened? Tell me if he . . . hurt you before he went off. Do you need a doctor?"

She began to cry like a child. "No!" she said. "No."

"Okay, good. Try to calm down, sweetheart. You'll be okay. Try to get hold of yourself so you can tell us what happened. Deidre? We'd better call his parents. Do you have his home phone?"

Curt moved convulsively in the corner, a flurry of motion like a trapped moth, shoving himself against the wall. A funny sound came from his throat. Then he fell silent and still again, breathing heavily.

"I think he's afraid of his father," Deidre said. "He's a violent man."

"Oh," said Jeff. "Okay, I see. All right, call nine one one. Tell them it's psychiatric, but we don't think the guy is dangerous. And make us some coffee." He turned back to Susie. "You sit down, honey," he said. "What's your name?"

Deidre went to the kitchen and called 911, explaining the situation. Then she started a pot of coffee, listening to Jeff and Susie in the living room, trying to sort out her feelings. She felt angry with him for giving her these menial orders to carry out, while he acted like God. She felt guilty for having such petty feelings during a major crisis. She felt jealous hearing him use all that honey and sweetheart stuff on Susie. She felt like a fool for what had happened earlier. She felt scared for Curt. She felt scared *of* Curt. She felt sorry for Susie. She felt relieved it had happened to Susie and not her. She felt guilty for having such a thought. She felt cheated that right now, when she wanted to play out her anger against Jeff, she had to cooperate with him in this larger drama. She wondered if she could get the beer stain off the wall before her mother came home. She took a wastebasket from under the sink and went back to the living room.

Susie was in a chair now, looking like a little girl in Jeff's big shirt. She sat with her hands up her sleeves. Jeff had taken a chair halfway between Susie and Curt. While Susie talked, he would throw little glances at Curt to make sure he wasn't doing anything.

"We shouldn't have been drinking, I know," Susie said. "It was just a couple of beers and I thought it wouldn't matter. But it made both of us . . . forget to be careful and we were . . . fooling around and I let him, I said, okay, we can take our tops off, just the tops, but then he wanted to do . . . the rest and he tried to take off my pants and I said stop! but he wouldn't stop and I got so angry because I was really scared of him, he always before would stop when I said stop but this time he wouldn't, he said, you don't really want me to, but I *did*. And I got so angry because I was scared and I started yelling and I forgot and I hit him. I hit him like five or six times really hard . . . because I was scared. I forgot I'm not supposed to."

Deidre, picking up beer cans and glass shards, explained. "We think he gets set off when somebody hits him because his dad . . ."

"Yeah, I see," Jeff said. "Combat fatigue."

Deidre finished picking up trash and sat down wearily. "The coffee's almost ready."

"Good. That's good. So did he hit you back, Susie? Or what did he do before he . . . checked out?"

"He just screamed," she said. Her eyes widened as she played the memory back. "He just clenched his fists and screamed. And he threw that glass of beer against the wall. He didn't even scream like a . . . man. It was like an animal. And then he sort of was shaking and . . . laughing. He was sort of laughing and he . . . it was like he started *shrinking*. He just backed away from me and he was like . . . pulling himself *in*. I can't explain. He just got into this tiny package on the floor and I called his name, but his eyes were empty. There was nobody there. And then you came in."

Deidre was amazed Susie was telling all this intimate stuff to Jeff. Susie, for all her chattering, was a private person. *Of course,* Deidre thought bitterly, *this is Jeff's talent. Getting people to open up and trust him, worming his way into the deepest, most secret part of them so he can stick a knife in. . . . This isn't the time for that,* she scolded herself. She got up and went to the kitchen to get the coffee.

That seemed to do everyone good. Susie was much calmer with a hot drink in her hands. "He looks so scary," she said, watching Curt, who was smiling faintly to himself.

"He's just . . . like I said, it happened to a friend of mine. They kind of . . . pull back when there's too much going on. You know what I mean? My friend came out of it okay. When they can handle reality again, they just sort of come back. At least that's what I think. But he should have psychiatric observation, especially if his dad is . . . a problem. Is he a minor?"

"Yes," Susie said.

"Well, good. They'll get HRS involved—"

There was a knock on the door.

"No! No!" Curt cried, pulling himself into a tight ball.

"Hey, Curt!" Jeff called. "It's okay, man. It's not your father. It's some people to protect you from him. All right?"

Curt made a whimpering sound.

Jeff opened the door. There were two paramedics and an old man in a cardigan sweater. All three briefly took in the room. Deidre was aware for the first time how bad the whole thing looked—an adult man with three teenagers, half the people topless or wearing the wrong shirts and the whole place smelling like a brewery.

"I'm Dr. Cleveland," the older man said, shaking Jeff's hand.

"Jeff Elliot. I'm a neighbor. The kids were having a party down here and Curt there kind of got set off and went on vacation. The girls tell me he's a battered child. He's kind of aware of what's going on but not really."

Deidre thought it was interesting Jeff's story made it sound like she'd been down here with the other kids instead of upstairs with him. He was obviously scared to have that known.

Dr. Cleveland went over and crouched by Curt. "Curt?" he said.

Curt blinked but gave no other sign.

"I'm Dr. Cleveland, Curt. I know you can hear me a little, can't you?"

Curt hugged himself tighter.

"We want to run over to the hospital and check you out and see how you are. Would that be okay?"

A sort of shudder went through Curt's body. His mouth worked, trying to say something. It was awful to watch, Deidre felt. Someone as bright and strong as Curt suddenly acting like a helpless baby. *"Dad,"* Curt finally croaked out as if naming a poison he had taken.

"How old is Curt?" Dr. Cleveland asked.

"Sixteen," Susie said.

"Any mother?"

"No."

The doctor turned back to Curt. "You don't have to

see your father at all. I can see to that. But I want you to come and sleep at the hospital tonight. That way you won't have to go home and all of us can look out for you."

Curt looked suddenly at Dr. Cleveland. It was the first eye contact he'd made with anyone. Tears began to run down his face, yet he wasn't crying or sobbing. It looked more like something was just leaking out of him.

Dr. Cleveland seemed to take that for consent. "Good boy," he said. He put his hand around Curt's waist. Curt neither helped nor resisted. They stood up together.

"Do you want me to go along?" Jeff asked. "For paperwork or something?"

"Do you know him well enough to fill out his admissions forms? That would help a lot."

"I don't know him at all," Jeff said. "This is the first time I've ever seen him."

"I'll go," Susie said. "I know his address and telephone and stuff, if that's what you want."

"Good. That way I don't have to deal with any . . . relatives until tomorrow."

"Is he going to be all right?" Susie asked, looking at Curt, who was leaning on the doctor's shoulder like an exhausted child.

"In all probability. This is usually a temporary reaction to a stress situation. Like a computer going down. He won't remain in this state probably for more than a few hours or days. Then, hopefully we can work on the causes."

Susie looked awkwardly at Deidre and Jeff. "Good night," she said. "Thanks for everything."

"Call me," Deidre said. "Do you want me to call Aunt Carol?"

"No. I'll call her from the hospital. She knew I was going to be here all night, so she won't worry."

"They can come with me in my car," Dr. Cleveland said to the paramedics, who had stood at the door like guard dogs. "No need for an ambulance. Good night, folks!" he said, as if leaving a pleasant Tupperware party. "Watch this step here," he said gently to Curt as they went out together.

"People like that are amazing," Jeff said, closing the door. "How does he do a job like that, day after day?"

Deidre sank down on the couch and put her hands over her face. It was too much. She didn't want to think anymore.

"You want me to go?" Jeff said after a pause.

She uncovered her eyes and looked at him standing there bare chested in her living room. *Who is that?* she wondered. A month ago she didn't even know him. What was he doing here now, all tangled and mixed up in her life? "Yes," she said flatly. "Go."

He took a step toward her. "I know you're tired," he said. "But maybe we should . . . talk. Do you want to go out to breakfast?"

Cruel. He was just cruel. Yesterday, she would have

killed for an invitation like that from him. He didn't seem to want to miss any chance to hurt her some more, rub her face in it. "I have a stain on my wall," she said, running her hands over her face. "I have to clean it."

He took another step. "Well, let me do that with you, then," he said. "I think—"

Deidre looked up. What really made her angry was that he was still attractive to her. Standing there so close with his shirt off. She wanted to kill him. "You've really done enough for one night!" she said, not trying to conceal the hostility now.

"Look, let's talk it out," he said, almost begging. "You've been through—"

Somehow Deidre found herself on her feet. Somehow her jaw was clenched so hard, it hurt her teeth at the roots. "Get out of here now!" she screamed. "And don't *ever* come back! I don't ever want to see you or think about you or hear your voice again! I mean it! Get OUT!" She literally shrieked the last word.

"Okay. I see," Jeff said quietly. He turned and left swiftly. The door closed again, a very final sound. And the apartment became an empty apartment again, with the clock ticking and the refrigerator humming. It was four A.M. Deidre collapsed on the couch and cried for twenty minutes, without even trying to think what she was crying about. Then she changed her clothes and cleaned the whole apartment, scrubbing the walls with white vinegar to take out the stain and then washing them with pine cleaner to take out the vinegar smell. She cleaned both bathrooms and changed all the sheets and towels. She ran the vacuum cleaner. She threw Susie's and Curt's T-shirts and Susie's bra in the trash with the broken glass and the empty beer cans. She found the rest of the six-pack in the refrigerator and threw that away too. Then she went to her bedroom and opened the night-table drawer. She took out two plastic swords, a match folder from the Holiday Inn, and her Billy Joel tape and added them all to the trash collection.

When she went outside to the incinerator chute, the sky was already growing light and the birds were awake, singing like idiots.

I

"Honey?" A gentle shake.

Her mother's voice. Deidre left her dream—something about green apples and a pie—and let her mind swim to the surface. She was lying on the couch and must have been sleeping heavily for hours. The room was full of bright sunshine.

Her mother, looking gritty and weary from her long car trip, sat on the edge of the couch, pushing back a limp strand of hair. She wore a wilted sundress and striped sandals and she was holding a large conch shell.

"What time is it?" Deidre yawned, struggling to sit up.

"Eleven-thirty. We just got back."

Deidre automatically glanced around the room. Everything was completely in order. No one would ever know two teenagers were drinking and making out here last night and that one of them went berserk. Deidre could almost believe the whole evening was unreal except for the heavy feeling on her chest that started the minute she realized she and Jeff were never going to happen.

"Where's Mr. Maxwell?" Deidre asked.

"He went on home. We were both pretty tired."

Deidre looked more closely at her mother now. It wasn't just road fatigue. Her eyes were red-rimmed and her hair wasn't just disheveled from the wind, it looked as if she'd been running nervous hands through it. "How'd the weekend go?" Deidre asked carefully.

"Okay," her mother said, much too quickly. "Look what I brought you. Put it up to your ear."

Deidre obediently listened to "the sea." "It's pretty. Did you get it on the beach?"

"No. They sell them. Are you hungry?"

The pressure on Deidre's chest said no. "I don't think so. I could use some coffee, though, maybe. How about you?"

Mrs. Holland smiled. "That," she said, "would be wonderful."

While Deidre made the coffee, feeling weird flashes of memory from the coffee she had made last night, Mrs. Holland took her suitcase back to the bedroom. When she came back she had brushed her hair, put on lipstick, and changed into a pretty housecoat. Deidre envied that. When she was depressed, she knew, she looked awful and no amount of "freshening up" would fix it. She supposed now she was going to look bedraggled for the rest of the summer. Or possibly the rest of her life.

No, she said to herself. *She wouldn't give Jeff that satisfaction. He wasn't worth it.* Happiness is a decision, she thought, a state of mind. She could talk herself out of this huge, horrible pressure inside her rib cage that was making it an effort to even inhale. She would focus on positive things: the warm, sunlit kitchen, the hot coffee, the pattern of daisies on her mother's housecoat. She would lose herself by thinking about someone else. "Tell the truth, Mom," she said. "What happened between you guys?"

Her mother looked up, alarmed. "It's nothing for *you* to worry about," she said.

"I want to worry about it. Believe me. Did you and Mr. Maxwell have a fight?"

"Sort of," she said, stirring even though she didn't use sugar.

"Big fight?"

"No. Well . . . yes."

"What was it about?"

Her mother looked up. "Deidre, this is an adult thing! I don't think I can discuss it with you!"

"Was it about sex?"

Her mother turned a lovely shade of pink, like the

inside of the conch shell. "No! Good heavens, no! That —that's the only thing we seem to agree about."

Deidre laughed. "Well, then, what? Does he leave the cap off the toothpaste?"

Her mother laughed. "No, he . . . do you really want to hear this?"

"Yes!"

"Well, he—he was just getting too *serious.* He was talking all about the future like we . . . like he expected . . . I mean, I never told him I'd marry him or anything and suddenly he's saying things about what size *house* we would need. So of course I had to tell him, look, let's just take this thing one day at a time. I mean, I like him—"

"Do you?" Deidre interrupted.

"What?"

Some whole new emotion was affecting Deidre now. She couldn't quite identify it, but it was even stronger than the heavy-chested feeling. It was pushing into her system like a thick flow of lava, shoving everything in its path aside. "Do you really like him? You never acted like you did!"

Her mother gave her an odd look. "Well, to be perfectly frank, there are quite a number of things I *don't* like about him. I don't think I could ever be serious about him. He's just not the type of man I . . . can go for. He—"

"Then why did you lead him on?" Deidre cried. Her

voice was loud and frightening. The emotion was clear now. It was rage.

Her mother blinked. "Lead him on? What do you—"

"Lead him on! That's what you did! First you chased after him, inviting him over for dinner, and anybody could see from the first time he was falling for you! But you couldn't care *less,* I guess! It's just somebody's *heart,* isn't it? How do you expect him to feel when you're always kissing and touching him and you spend the night with him and then you go away with him for a whole weekend? Didn't you think that might make somebody fall in love with you? Couldn't you see it in his eyes? *I* could see it. I was even thinking how nice he'd be as a stepfather. He's one of the nicest men I've ever met! I don't know what kind of a John Wayne you think you're holding out for, but I think Mr. Maxwell is a *wonderful* person who cares about you. Isn't that good enough for you? Someone who would love you and be good to you and take care of you? What else do you want?"

Mrs. Holland had become absolutely still. "Deidre, what's gotten into you? You've never talked to me that way before!"

"That doesn't mean I can't!" Deidre raved. "It's a free country!" She realized how awful she sounded, but she couldn't control herself. The emotion inside her was too big to hold down.

Mrs. Holland had tears in her eyes. "I didn't realize how much you wanted a father!"

"It's not about that!" Deidre shouted. "I'm not thinking about me! I'm thinking about him! He was a nice man! That day we went to the park he told me how much he loved you! Doesn't that count for anything?"

"No!" her mother cried. "It doesn't! Not if I don't love him back! I'm not *obligated* by the fact he loves me. I don't have to love him just because he's *nice!* Lots of people are nice! So what?"

"So you leave them alone, then, and don't let them get involved with you!"

"I didn't know how I felt at first. It took time!"

"Don't you care what you're doing to him?"

"Why are you on *his* side? *I'm* your mother!"

Deidre was near tears. "Because!" she shouted. "People like you don't realize . . . to you it's just a game, but you can wreck another person's whole life while you're fooling around and deciding and making up your mind."

"What do you want me to do?" her mother cried. "Marry someone I don't love just so he won't get hurt?"

Deidre got up from the table, stumbling and knocking her chair over. "I just think all the people like you should be put on some kind of island somewhere, so you can't hurt the rest of us!"

Her mother was angry now too. Her eyes were flashing. "Nobody, not even you, is going to make me feel guilty for something I can't help! It's not my fault that I don't love him!"

The tears began to run down Deidre's face in hot

streams. Tremors coursed up and down the backs of her legs. "But don't you see?" she pleaded. "It's your fault that *he* loves *you*!" Then the urge to cry was so overwhelming, she had to run from the room like a child and lock herself in her bedroom. She sobbed in horrible gulps and gasps. It took almost an hour before she felt calm again. But as soon as she did, she got up and combed her hair and went back to the living room.

Her mother was sitting on the couch, marking up the classified ads. She looked up warily.

"I just wanted to tell you I'm sorry," Deidre said. "I didn't really mean any of that. What I was doing . . . I was really saying all that stuff to someone else. You know what I mean?"

Her mother looked down. "Yes," she said. "I was doing the same thing."

· **15** ·

Deidre lay on her back in the hall, reading the warnings on the smoke detector. *Important! Read owner's manual BEFORE installation! See reverse side for more information. Smoke detector will not operate if battery is dead, disconnected, or improperly installed!* Life was full of hazards, all right.

She had been living in the hall for two days, watching the angles of sunlight shift around the house, waiting for some kind of miraculous recovery from the depression she felt. She had always liked the vaulted, protective feeling in the hall. When she was a little girl, her mother had told her to go to the hall if there was a hurricane warning, because it was *the safest place in the house.* Ever since, Deidre had used it as a personal cave, a private sanctuary to crawl into when things got rough. And of course, it was also the best place in the house for listening to the music upstairs.

Today, he'd been playing off and on since two. She

imagined he was playing softer these past few days, as if he knew she could hear him and felt embarrassed about it. He never played the rhapsody. Maybe he had junked it. Deidre listened to his selections almost against her will, trying to pick out clues to his state of mind. Today he had played "Tears of a Clown," "Before My Very Eyes," "It Takes Two," "Out of Touch," and "Kissing a Fool." Were these messages to her? she wondered.

Then she would scold herself. That was the kind of thinking that had got her into this mess. He probably wasn't thinking of her at all. The whole terrible night of his birthday, which Deidre now had nightmares about, was probably a baffling minor incident to him. She could imagine him telling Nicki, the bartender, about it. "You know that crazy kid who came in here a couple of times? You'll never believe what she tried to pull. . . ."

Deidre rolled over and put her face in her hands, to blot it out. The music upstairs stopped abruptly.

Then the telephone rang.

Deidre froze. It rang again. Her heart hammered in her chest. Slowly, she got up and began to walk toward the kitchen, keeping her eyes on the phone as if it were a snake. Patiently, the phone rang and rang as if the caller knew Deidre was there and was determined to wait her out. What if he apologized? What if he asked her to come up? What if he begged her forgiveness and told her he'd been a fool not to realize his true feelings?

"Hello?" Deidre whispered into the phone.

"Where were you? On the john?"

"Susie," Deidre said flatly.

"Yeah. Did the beer come off the wall?"

"Yes. How are you doing?"

"Oh. I'm all right. The reason I called is I just talked to the hospital where Curt is and I thought you'd want to know. . . ."

"Yes! How is he?"

"Stable. In stable condition. I finally got the doctor, you know, the old guy that came over and he said Curt was . . . you know, back with us . . . and that he was going to *rest* a few weeks in the hospital. Then he'll be an outpatient. The doctor said there has to be a court hearing about his dad. He might lose custody, but I don't know where Curt would go. . . . Well, anyway, the main thing is, he's back from La-la Land, so—"

"When are you going over?"

"Huh?"

"When are you going to the hospital? Because, if it's okay with you, I'd like to go along. I like Curt and—"

"I don't think I'm going to do that," Susie said in an odd voice.

"You're going to wait until he's released? I thought you said—"

"Dee. I haven't decided if I want to see him at *all*. I mean, it was a big deal for me just going *in* one of those places, the night they admitted him. Just now calling them gave me the creeps. I wouldn't have even done that, but I had to know . . . you know, if he was still in that state. But—"

"Susie! Are you saying you would dump this guy just because he had a little—"

"He didn't have a little anything! He had a *big.* And the word is breakdown. Nervous breakdown. I mean, I can't handle—"

"Don't you care about him?"

"Look, it's easy for you to say. It didn't happen to you. He scared the—excuse me—shit out of me. I'll never forget his eyes when he was throwing that glass against the wall. . . . How do I know that would never happen again? Maybe his dad screwed him up permanently."

"But you . . . when you care about somebody, you don't just—"

"Deidre. I'm really tired of hearing that kind of stuff from you."

"What kind of stuff?"

"All the stuff about what love is and what it isn't and how you're supposed to act if you care about someone . . . what do *you* know about it? You don't know *anything.* Because you haven't been through it!"

"How can you say that? You know how I feel about Jeff and now he—"

"Deidre! That's not real! You *know* it's not. It never could be. He's a grown man. You don't really know him at all. He's just . . . like a rock star or an actor. I mean, you've really got a lot of nerve, preaching to me about being too scared to deal with stuff. You're the chicken! That's why you picked Jeff out. Because deep down, you *know* it can't happen so you can do the whole thing in your *mind* and be *safe—*"

"Shut up!" Deidre shouted. Then she did something she'd never done before. She hung up on someone. Even that wasn't good enough. She picked up the receiver and slammed it down again. Then she unplugged the phone and put it in a drawer.

But it didn't do any good.

Deidre hugged herself, drifting back toward the hall, trying not to think, but thinking anyway. She thought about that scared, panicky feeling she got when she saw her mother and Mr. Maxwell together, or Curt and Susie. It was true. When she met Jeff she had known he'd be safe, that he'd give her all the warmth and affection she wanted, because that was what he was like. But no real danger. No chance of anything really happening. She had used him to practice her romantic feelings on. She had used him.

She remembered the angry things he'd said that night in his apartment. He *felt* used. And he didn't know the half of it! What if he'd found out the way she went through his things, touched his underwear, read his letters? What if he knew how she'd kissed him that night, when he wasn't even conscious? How would she feel if someone did that to her?

The music began to play again. "What's Love Got to

Do with It?" Good question. One that deserved an answer. Deidre went to look for her shoes.

I

He opened the door looking hopeful, expecting someone else. Then he saw Deidre and looked wary. "Hi."

"Hi," she said. "Can I come in?"

"Sure. Always." He stepped back to let her pass. "You want something to drink?"

She paused in the hall. "Is it pineapple juice?"

"Yes. That's all I have that's not alcoholic."

"I really don't *like* pineapple juice."

"No? Well . . . would you mind if I had a beer? I feel sort of—"

"You don't have to ask *my* permission."

"No. I know. Sit down. I'm really glad you came up, because there's something I want to say to you."

"Me too." She went to the living room while he got his beer. Cyril was lying on the piano. She went and petted him. He purred and rolled over. It was the first time he'd ever been nice to her.

Jeff came in, taking rapid sips as if he wanted to get the alcohol into his bloodstream fast. He wore an aqua shirt today that made his coloring look a little harsh. Too brassy. His eyes were scared. "What I want to do is apologize to you," he said. "For . . . everything, but especially for Friday night. I got upset and acted . . .

I'm not a bad person, really. I just didn't understand . . ."

"I know all that." Deidre waved her hand. "I came up to apologize to you."

He perched on the rocking horse and took another healthy slug from the can. "What for? You've been like a little angel to me. I've never met anyone as nice as you."

"Well, thanks, but it's not . . . you were right about some of the things you said. I was nice to you because . . . well, you know, I was trying to get somewhere with you, so it wasn't like . . . I'm not a saint or anything. I'm just stupid."

"You're not stupid. *I'm* stupid. I was the adult here. Any normal guy would have seen what was going on with you and stopped it, or said something. But I'm always so dense. I never pick up on anything. Or maybe I didn't want to because, frankly, I was very lonely and feeling sorry for myself and it was just really . . . *handy* to have this wonderful person bringing me food and talking to me and telling me I was such a big shot. You're so good for my ego, sweetheart. And my ego was in bad shape when I met you. So I feel like I used you."

"We used each other," Deidre said. "I needed some kind of fantasy guy that was too perfect to be real."

"Oh, well, I can see how you chose me for *that*," he joked. "So we used each other. Hey. What are friends for?"

"That's right." Deidre smiled. "You can use me any-time."

"Same here. What happened to your friends? The guy? Is he okay?"

"It looks like he probably will be."

"Good. Good." He gulped the rest of the beer and set it down.

"How are things going for you?" Deidre asked. "Are you going to get back together with Chrissie?"

He flinched. "What would make you say that?"

Deidre had to think fast. She didn't want him to ever know the way she'd invaded his privacy. "The way you answered the door," she explained. "You looked like you were expecting somebody else."

"Boy! You are so perceptive! I called her last night. We talked. She said she might come over later today. Does it bother you to talk about this?"

"No," Deidre said, and strangely, it didn't. "Did you get anything settled?"

"No, but we got somewhere, I think. We agreed about the fact we missed each other and that's the im-portant thing. I really . . . love her."

Deidre realized some part of her had known this all along. It was another thing that made him safe. "If she's coming over, I'd better go."

"No, wait!" he said, almost shyly. "The rhapsody's finished. Can I play it for you?"

She pulled her feet up, getting comfortable. "Of course."

"Great." He started toward the piano, then hesitated. "I want to explain something before I play it. It's about . . . you and this piece of music. I mean, I'm a stupid idiot and a clod and I can't express myself at all but . . . the reason I was able to write this is because . . . *you* came along and inspired it. It's about *you*. The way you make me feel. The minute I gave it your name I started making breakthroughs. Because you have this quality about you that's so . . . special. . . . Okay, that's enough of that crap. Just listen to it."

He sat down and began to play. The music slowly swirled out and filled the room. It was sad, there was a recurring note of sadness, but a sweetness too. And an incredible feeling of gentleness. He saw all of that in her. Maybe someday some other man would see the same things in Deidre and it would turn into love. This time it had turned into music. And friendship.

When Jeff was finished, he turned around for her verdict, anxious as a child, and she jumped up and ran to put her arms around him. "Beautiful!" she said.

ABOUT THE AUTHOR

JOYCE SWEENEY was born in Dayton, Ohio. She attended Wright State University and did graduate work at Ohio University. Her first book, *Center Line,* won the First Annual Delacorte Press Prize for an Outstanding First Young Adult Novel. Joyce Sweeney is also the author of *Right Behind the Rain, The Dream Collector,* and *Face the Dragon.* She works as a free-lance book critic and columnist for the *Fort Lauderdale Sun-Sentinel.* She lives in Coral Springs, Florida, with her husband, Jay, and cat, Macoco.